*DARK
MYSTERIOUS
HE SEEMED TO MOVE IN THE
SHADOWS AND THEN . . .*

He made some inarticulate sound and, covering the distance between them in a single stride, swept her into his arms. She came readily to his embrace, and for a long time they clung together as though they would never part. The door opened, and Lady Chalfont came into the room. She stopped on the threshold unable to believe the sight before her eys. . . .

Beloved Diana

Alice Chetwynd Ley

BALLANTINE BOOKS • NEW YORK

ISBN 0-345-25612-3

Manufactured in the United States of America

First Ballantine Books Edition: November 1977

CONTENTS

1

A Stranger Comes to Chesdene

THE TRAVELLER cast an experienced eye over the pleasant, low-ceilinged room, then crossed to the window to stand for a moment looking down on the broad, tree-lined street of the little country town.

A chilly wind had sprung up, setting the signboards swinging on the row of small shops opposite and driving idle strollers within doors. A farm cart came rumbling slowly past, followed by two small boys. As he watched, they attempted to scramble up on to the tailboard; but the carter shouted at them, flicking his whip in warning, and they quickly desisted. A smile lightened the somewhat austere face of the traveller. The incident carried him back, as so much did at the moment, to an earlier period of his life; to a period which for many years he had tried to forget.

He turned to the landlord of the King's Arms, who was waiting respectfully by the door.

"This will do. Have a horse saddled and waiting outside the inn for me in ten minutes."

The landlord stared. This gentleman had only that moment stepped down from a dusty post chaise and bespoken a room at the inn. At the very least he must have come from London, a distance of some thirty miles, and now here he was wanting to set off on his travels again.

"Will ye be going far, y'r honour?" he ventured to ask. "Looks uncommon like rain."

The traveller favoured him with a hard stare which made him shuffle his feet awkwardly.

"I shall return here to dine at six."

The landlord began to recite the menu, but his guest cut him short. "Anything will do. I leave it to you."

A nod, and the landlord was dismissed. He took himself downstairs to see about the horse, wondering as he did so who his guest might be.

Except for coaches pausing on long-distance journeys, few travellers came to the town to stay unless they had business here. This one did not look like a man of business. He had a hard, tanned face which suggested an outdoor life; while the upright carriage and decisive manner might well belong to a military or naval officer. Plenty of those about, thought the landlord, with this war on against Boney which kept prices so high that a poor innkeeper had a job to make a worthwhile living. By nature of his calling, the landlord was a shrewd judge of men, and he knew that here was one whom it would not pay to cross. In spite of the casual way in which the dinner had been ordered, he intended to see that the meal was the best the house could provide. Payment? No need to worry there; that authoritative manner did not spring from empty pockets, if he knew anything of men.

Precisely ten minutes later, the traveller came down and mounted the horse which was waiting outside the inn door.

He rode down the street until the houses dwindled and he came to open country, with only an occasional farmstead in view. It was late March; the wind was cold, but he did not heed it, looking about him with that keen, dark eye which had so disconcerted the landlord of the King's Arms, and which seemed to miss nothing.

The trees were putting forth their first timid tips of green; here and there in the hedgerows an occasional pale primrose showed, or a cluster of violets. He had forgotten how busy all nature was at this season; lambs bleated in the meadows, a foal nuzzled its mother, birds flitted briskly from branch to branch, twittering ceaselessly. Even though grey clouds scudded across the sky and misted the Chiltern Hills, they could not dull the sudden, fierce leap of exultation within him. This was his country, he thought with a quick surge of possession; and, by God, there was no other country in the world to touch it—England in the Spring.

As if to mock him, the rain came, drifting softly in the wind so that he was scarcely conscious of it. He kept to the main road for a few miles, then turned off into a narrow lane which wound downhill, bordered by low hedges. After a time, a few cottages came into view, scattered at first, but grouped more closely together as the lane descended more and more steeply until it reached the village of Chesdene.

At the foot of the hill he drew rein, gazing at the ancient village which clustered about a large green shaded by elms. A young girl was drawing water from the well in the middle of the green, and a flock of geese hissed round her bare feet. She was the only inhabitant to be seen apart from an old man in a dirty smock who loitered outside the village tavern, the Red Lion. The smoking cottage chimneys, however, suggested plenty of activity within doors. A dog nosed at the gate of one of the cottages and pushed it open, trotting confidently up the path as though certain of its welcome. Something in the sight brought a wry twist to the watcher's mouth. He jerked suddenly at the horse's rein, urging it towards the path which ran across the green to join a stony track on the opposite side. This led to the church, a fifteenth century building of grey flint; just beyond the church tower, the tall twisted chimneys of Chesdene Manor appeared above the high wall which screened the house from view.

As he rode past the well, the geese moved menacingly towards him, screaming in anger. His horse shied in alarm, but he curbed it with a firm hand. The girl at the well set down her pail and, seizing a stick, ran forward to shoo the geese from his path. He tossed her a coin as he continued on his way, and she stood for a moment staring after him, for nowadays strangers seldom came to Chesdene.

When he reached the church he dismounted, tethering his horse to a post beside the lych gate. The animal at once began to crop an unexpected patch of grass which grew there, while its rider continued along the track on foot.

It was only a short distance to the Manor. Although a high wall surrounded it, the entrance gates were of ornamental wrought iron which afforded an almost uninterrupted view of the house. Having first ascertained by a quick glance that no one was about in the forecourt, he stood close to the gates, his face pressed against the interstices of the ironwork, gazing at the house.

It was an L-shaped building, most of which had been grafted in Tudor times on to a somewhat incongruous grey stone tower; all that remained of an earlier mediaeval house. The longer wing, to his left, was beautiful, of mellow red brick with tall, twisted chimneys and mullioned windows. Immediately in front of him was the shorter north wing; this was of more recent date, with stucco facing, sash windows and a pillared portico.

He drew a deep breath like one who is under some strong emotional stress, and for a long time stood motionless at the gates, staring as if his very existence depended on it.

At last he stirred. His keen eyes had noticed that the door behind the portico was opening. As he drew quickly back from the gate to the shelter of the wall he saw two female figures emerging, both wearing cloaks and one of them carrying an umbrella.

Taking care to keep out of a direct line with the gates, he strode swiftly back to the church. He passed by his horse, which was still cropping contentedly, and went through the lych gate and down the path to the church door. He entered the porch and removed his beaver hat, shaking the rain from it.

The interior of the church was dim, but he did not

miss the two steps which led down into it. He walked towards the altar, his footsteps ringing on the stone floor. With the air of one long unaccustomed, he bowed his head for a moment, then turned to study the alabaster monument which dominated the north wall. It showed two kneeling figures, a man and a woman, and the Latin inscription underneath showed that this was the tomb of Sir John Chalfont and his wife Agnes, who died in 1443.

He walked slowly back up the chancel and nave towards the door by which he had entered. On his way he passed many memorials dedicated to the memory of Chalfonts who had died in past centuries; but the one before which he finally paused was a cartouche tablet, of more recent date, bearing the name of Sir John Chalfont, Baronet, who departed this life in 1796.

"He was a tender husband, loving parent, and a wise and just master to all who served him. His multitudinous virtues and sterling piety were an example to his neighbours, and live on in the memory of his sorrowing family."

As he read the fulsome words, an unpleasant expression came over his lean face, giving it a hawk-like appearance. He jerked back his head, emitting a short, harsh laugh which held no trace of amusement and which in that place seemed almost an act of sacrilege.

He turned away with quickened step to the door. As he emerged into the porch, he nearly collided with two ladies who were about to enter the church. With a muttered apology, he drew back against the wall so that they could pass. One of them stopped to set down an umbrella which she was carrying. The other paused to wait for her, and for a moment turned a frank, curious look upon the stranger, which he met with a level gaze. He noticed that she was young, about twenty, with clear hazel eyes, set in a fine-featured face; the hair which showed from beneath the hood of her cape was brown and glowed with reddish tints. He looked from her to her companion, a girl of much the same age or perhaps a little younger, who was shorter and more fragile looking, with pretty blonde hair and blue eyes.

Having taken one quick look at him, the young ladies modestly averted their eyes and passed by to enter the church.

He remained standing for a moment in the shelter of the porch, deep in thought. At length he roused himself and stepped out into the rain to make his way purposefully down a path at the west side which led to the graveyard. Here were many more Chalfont tombs, but he paid scant heed to any of them, until he came to a simple stone without eulogy or embellishment which stood close beside the enclosing wall of the graveyard.

The rain fell more sharply now, but he seemed unconscious of it, in spite of the fact that he was still bare-headed. For a long time he stood motionless before the grave, his face drained of expression.

He was roused at last by a neigh from his horse and the scrape of an impatient hoof. He shrugged his shoulders, seemed suddenly to recollect his hat and crammed it on his head, then went with quickened step to the lych gate.

Once in the saddle, he rode back by the way he had come, drawing rein at the Red Lion, where he gave the horse into the care of a lad who was working in the stables at the rear of the inn.

He made his way round to the front again, ducking his head as he entered the door, for the Red Lion had been built in earlier times, with low doorways and ceilings. The door opened straight into the taproom, often gloomy enough by reason of its heavy oak beams and small diamond paned windows which admitted little light. Today, however, the dim interior was enlivened by the flickering light of a cheerful fire on the wide hearth. Beside this in the inglenook sat the old man whom the traveller had previously noticed outside the inn. Evidently he had somehow managed to find the price of a pint of ale, for he held a tankard in his hand and was slowly drinking from it as he gazed with rheumy eyes into the fire.

He nodded and touched his hat to the stranger, who briefly returned the courtesy as he strode to the counter. The landlord appeared promptly behind it, and asked how he could serve his new customer.

"Ale," replied the stranger, briefly, flinging down a coin.

"Pesky ol' weather, sir," commented the landlord, as he drew a foaming-tankard and placed it on the counter. "Come on real hard, now, it has, for sure. Ye'll be passin' through, likely, sir?"

The traveller contented himself with a nod before raising the tankard and taking a deep draught from it.

This could scarcely have been considered as an invitation to further conversation, but the landlord was a persistent man. Like most village innkeepers, he was curious about the doing of others. It was simple enough to keep himself well informed as far as the local inhabitants were concerned, but strangers were infrequent, and offered more of a challenge.

"Ah," he said, in an easy tone. "Just so. I thought mebbe y'r honour might've come about the Manor, though."

The stranger lifted an eyebrow, but made no comment. If the landlord was disappointed, he did not show it, but proceeded to give the explanation which had not been demanded.

"Chesdene Manor," he continued, leaning his arms on the counter in the attitude of one about to embark on a prolonged gossip. "By what I do 'ear, ladies there be lookin' for a tenant. In course, rightly the house belongs to the new baronet, Sir Sidney Chalfont; but 'is honour's no mind to live there himself, and who's to blame 'im? A fair ol' state that place is in nowadays, and Sir Sidney—so they say—not wishful to lay out 'is blunt on settin' it to rights, on account o' bein' none too plump in the pocket 'imself. So seemingly he's given the ladies leave to stay on there, and raises no objection if they let off part o' the house to someone else." He shook his head sadly. "Ay, things was different in old Sir John's time! Then the Manor and the estate was all as trim an' spruce as a place should be that's housed gentlefolk for I dunno 'ow many hundreds o' years. Reckon Sir John 'ad precious little joy o' his sons, arter all; for young Mr. Ralph married to disoblige 'im, an' Mr. Peter—Sir Peter that's been gone these two years—gamed away nigh on all the Chalfont money, as everyone in these parts knows. Ah, well, I allus says as it's easier to get rid o' money than to make it, what say ye, sir?"

But the stranger still refused to be drawn. He considered the landlord thoughtfully for a few moments, then drained his tankard and slapped it down on the counter. Beside it he placed another coin, indicating with a jerk of his head the old man in the inglenook.

"Good day," he said, brusquely, as he strode from the inn.

The landlord stared resentfully after him. "Well, there's a talkative cove, if ye likes!" he commented to his only other customer. "No 'arm in passin' the time o' day, now, is there?"

The old man cackled, revealing a few blackened stumps of teeth. "Doan't 'ardly get much o' a chance wi' ye about, Joe Astill, do 'e? But I'll say no 'arm on 'im, seein' as 'e's left me the price o' another pot. Let's be 'aving it, then."

2

THE LADIES OF CHESDENE MANOR

"OF COURSE," remarked Diana Chalfont reflectively, "we might turn the place into a school."

Lady Chalfont looked up from her embroidery, a

startled expression on her face. "A school, my love?"

"Yes—you know, Mama, a girls' seminary. It's a healthful situation here, plenty of fresh air and country walks, and good wholesome food, not like that sadly adulterated stuff they often get in London. And we're not too far from London, either. That would be an advantage. Of course, we should have to start in quite a small way at first," she continued, warming to her theme, "but if people were satisfied, they would tell others, and in that way we should soon build up a respectable connection."

"A *school*," repeated Lady Chalfont, giving the word an emphasis which suggested that it was some outlandish invention. "But pray where would we find the teachers, for we could not afford to employ any?"

"We would do the teaching ourselves," replied Diana, absently. Her quick mind was considering other details.

Her mother's mouth fell slightly open and the needle she had been holding slipped from her grasp.

"Ourselves?" she echoed, in faltering tones. "Oh, my dear, how could we possibly attempt anything of the kind? I am sure *I* have positively no talent for the art of instruction! Of course, I know you are prodigiously clever, and perhaps might teach the little ones to read and write—"

"More than that I hope," replied her daughter with energy. "Perhaps we could not quite aspire to rival Mrs. Masquerier's establishment in Kensington, but we might make a push to offer almost as many subjects as she does. I speak French, and both of us are reasonably well versed in the foremost English writers. Some arithmetic, the use of the globes—a female needs very little of that kind of thing, after all—music and dancing. As for needlework, my dear Mama, no one could be more expert than you are yourself, I am sure. Deportment and manners, too—there you would excel! Oh, no, teachers would not be a difficulty at all, as far as I can see. The only hindrance is—" she broke off, and sighed—"we could not possibly accommodate more than one or two pupils in this part of the house that we occupy ourselves; and I must confess that I am completely at a stand to think of a way of bringing the rest of it into any kind of order that would satisfy the least exacting of parents!"

"No," replied Lady Chalfont with evident relief. "No, there is nothing to be done about that without money, and we have barely enough for our needs as it is. Besides, I dare say Sir Sidney would not permit it." She paused to retrieve her needle, but did not continue with her work for a moment. "If only," she said, with an echo of her daughter's sigh, "your poor Papa had not been so fatally addicted to gambling."

"There's no earthly use in saying that, Mama." There was a trace of impatience in Diana's tone. "It can alter nothing. What we must do is to contrive as best we can. At least we have a roof over our heads, which is something to be thankful for, and the new heir does not seem to mind if we try to turn the house to good account. And though the rest may be shabby and neglected, our own quarters are quite snug, you must admit."

"Oh yes, indeed, we are very comfortable here. Though I do think we should try for some new furnishings in the parlour. The green hangings are quite faded; I noticed it yesterday, when the sun was out, particularly."

Diana shrugged. "The spring sunshine always shows up the faults in one's furnishings. Well, I will see what can be done; although I don't promise—unless Mr. Dally does manage to find a tenant for us. I haven't entirely despaired of that notion, yet."

Lady Chalfont sighed. "I can't think it would be very pleasant, my love, to live at such close quarters with another family, particularly one with whom we're not even acquainted."

"Nonsense, Mama! This wing is quite shut off from the rest of the house, with its separate entrance and even our own private garden, although it *is* small."

"Yes, it was a good thing for us that the dowager

Lady Chalfont of the time had this wing built on for her own use when her son took a bride, some fifty or so years ago. It was in much better condition than the older part of the house when we were obliged to leave London and finally settle here, and by then your poor Papa certainly hadn't the means to set the whole place in order. Of course, he should have settled here when your Grandfather died, by rights, and then the Manor would never have become so dilapidated—eight years is a long time to leave a house empty, especially such an old house as this. But there!" She sighed again. "It is always difficult to know in advance what is best to be done. Your Papa always detested the country, and even when your Grandfather was alive, I had the utmost difficulty in persuading him to leave London to pay the old man a visit, now and then."

"It wasn't only that he disliked the country, though, was it?" asked Diana. "From what you have told me, Mama, I collect that he was made uncomfortable by the way Grandfather treated my Aunt Amelia. Of course, I don't remember her at all, nor my cousin Robert."

"How should you, my love? You were only six when she died. Yes, it's quite true that your Papa hated to see her used as she was; but, all the same, he could not very well—" she broke off, obviously embarrassed. "Your Grandfather had a most uncertain temper," she continued, after a pause, "and Peter—your Papa—was dependent on him, after all. But I must confess I have sometimes wondered if—if perhaps we could not have done something to make that poor woman's life less of a burden. The boy, Robert, you know, said as much when there was that dreadful quarrel on the day of his Mother's funeral—poor boy! One must not speak ill of the dead, I know, but your Grandfather did taunt him so, and at such a time, when the lad was near distracted with grief at his Mother's loss! Small wonder that poor young Robert turned on us all, and swore to be avenged for the treatment meted out to his Mother."

"As for speaking ill of the dead," said Diana, forcefully, "it seems to me that a man's actions during his lifetime are not rendered any more praiseworthy by the fact of his death. By all accounts, my Grandfather must have been a perfect fiend!"

"Hush, dear, you must not say so. He had great pride in the family name, in the Manor and all it stood for. Indeed, these were the ruling passions of his life. And so when your Uncle Ralph eloped with this girl who had neither family nor fortune, instead of making the brilliant match which had been planned for him, it almost broke your Grandfather's heart. And after all one must give him credit for taking in Amelia and her little son after poor Ralph's tragic death at so early an age."

"Credit!" repeated Diana, bitterly. "Much credit it was to take his revenge on a helpless woman and child, for that is what he did! No, Mama, you should not stop me from saying so! It's of no use to tell me I was too young to form any judgment about it—that's true, of course, but I have heard enough from you since, on several occasions, to show me exactly how things were."

She did not voice another opinion she held, which was that her father ought to have intervened at whatever cost to himself. Hers was a frank and fearless nature, and she found it hard to understand how anyone could stand by without protest and see an injustice done. Only one thing could ever keep her from speaking her mind, and that was affection for another. It was for her Mother's sake that she said no more now.

It would not have been easy to foresee the family's present difficulties twelve years ago, when Sir John Chalfont died. He had left the entailed Manor and a considerable fortune to his only surviving son, Peter. All the world knew that Peter Chalfont was a dedicated gambler, but so were most other gentlemen who moved within his own fashionable circle in London. At first, Sir John had thought little of his son's expensive pastimes, believing that time and the steadying influence of a wife and family would eventually eradicate them.

Meanwhile, Sir John had held the purse strings, and could see to it that his wild young heir did not seriously impair the family funds. But in the years just before his death a different mood overcame him, and he often wondered who would keep Peter in check when he had gone, and what would become of little Diana, who now looked like being his sole grandchild.

His uneasiness was justified. As soon as Peter Chalfont became Sir Peter and the keeper of his own purse, his wildness increased. Gradually the fortune dwindled and he was forced to realise what assets he could from the Chesdene estate; timber was ruthlessly felled and sold, together with livestock and any land not under entail. Nothing was spent on upkeep, and the Manor itself was shut up and placed in the sole charge of an elderly caretaker. Matters went from bad to worse in spite of protests from the family lawyer, Mr. Dally, protests which at last were echoed by Sir Peter's wife, who feared for the fortune of her young daughter. Sir Peter laughed this off, saying that such a pretty girl would certainly make a good match; and he continued gaily on his downward course.

The climax came in 1804, when his father had been dead for eight years. He was obliged at last to sell up the London house, his smart carriages and fine bred horses; to dismiss most of his staff, and retire to the despised Manor at Chesdene. By that time, the main part of the house was showing the effects of long years of neglect, and improvements would have involved a considerable outlay.

Because it was not so old, the Dowager's wing had, however, suffered less than the rest of the house, and was more easily brought into some kind of order. It was deemed large enough for the family's present needs, especially in view of their depleted staff, which now consisted of a cook-housekeeper who managed all the domestic affairs with the help of a girl who came in daily from the village; and the housekeeper's husband, who acted as gardener, handyman and stable boy. His duties in the latter capacity took up very little of his

time, for of all their once magnificent stable, the Chalfonts only managed to retain one tolerable horse for Sir
Peter himself and a broken-winded mare for Miss Diana to ride. They had no carriage, but later purchased
a rickety gig at a local farm sale.

Having settled his family in this impoverished style
in the depths of Buckinghamshire and away from all
their former acquaintances, Sir Peter left them more or
less to their own devices while he ranged here and
there on protracted visits to those of his former friends
who could still be persuaded to offer him hospitality.
As these gentlemen all shared his passion for gambling,
his visits did nothing to restore the family fortunes; on
the contrary, they were a constant drain on what little
was left. One by one, the elegancies which remained
were pared away.

When things had reached this pass, Sir Peter showed
the first good sense of his life by quitting it before his
family were thrown on the parish as paupers. On one
of his visits from home, he broke his neck in a carriage
race which would have brought him a thousand
guineas if he had won it. His wife and daughter mourn-
ed him sincerely, a fact which says much for their loving dispositions.

The funeral was attended by Lady Chalfont's
brother, a man of unswerving rectitude who had
viewed from a distance with deep disapproval the activities of his erratic brother-in-law. As head of his
family, he magnanimously offered to receive his sister
and niece into his own household when the new heir
should take possession of Chesdene Manor. His prim
wife screwed up her thin lips on hearing this but said
nothing, mindful of her duty as a Christian. She also
reminded herself that her sister-in-law had always been
good with her needle, and dressmakers were an expensive item when one had two young daughters. Her
niece Diana, too, although not a girl she could at all
approve of in a general way, spoke French very prettily
and had some talent for music. Melinda and Sarah
would go to a good Young Ladies Seminary in a few

years' time, of course; but meanwhile Governesses *were* expensive . . .

She need not have troubled her head with these reflections; for, prompted by Diana, Lady Chalfont had gently but firmly refused her brother's offer, saying she preferred to keep her own household as long as she possibly could.

"I wish you may be able to do so, sister," he had replied, gravely, "but I greatly fear that when you hear what the lawyer has to say, you may find there is even less for you than you suppose. Everything must go to the new baronet, you know, except for your own small settlements; and if he chooses to turn you out of the Manor, he is quite within his rights, so that you could well find yourself without even a roof over your head. It is perhaps a pity," he added, reflectively, "that your young nephew didn't live to inherit. He could not very well have turned you out, but this man is no very close kin, and scarcely known to you."

"That poor boy," replied Lady Chalfont, her tears starting afresh. "And his poor dear Mama! We ought to have done more to help them, indeed I feel it—but Sir John was ever a difficult man, and my husband—" she choked a little—"never dared to antagonise his father by urging anything on their behalf."

"Ah well, there is no need to distress yourself over that, my dear Andrea. It is long since gone by, and you have troubles enough of your own at hand. I suppose that for form's sake your lawyer will insert advertisements in the newspapers before handing over the inheritance to your kinsman Mr. Sidney Chalfont; but there can be no doubt at all that young Robert Chalfont perished fourteen years ago when the ship that was carrying him to Portugal sank in the Bay of Biscay."

"And even if he had not," Diana had retorted, somewhat acidly, "one cannot suppose that the temptation to secure such an inheritance as a neglected estate would prove very strong."

"There is the title," her uncle reminded her.

"From all I've ever heard, he must have loathed the very name of Chalfont," was Diana's comment. "And I can't say I for one blame him."

Speaking once more of these past events had brought a tear to Lady Chalfont's eye, and her voice was tremulous when next she spoke.

"Ah well, it is all long since gone by. But I often wonder what is to become of the old house in the end, for it's plain to see our kinsman hasn't the means to make the necessary repairs and renovations to keep it going for the next generation. I've heard it rumoured, my love—" she lowered her voice, though there was no one to overhear them—"that Sir Sidney is as given to gambling as your poor Papa was, and with an equal lack of success."

"Well, he's a Chalfont, after all, and by all accounts it's a family weakness. I sometimes wonder if I shall not turn out to be tainted with it, too—not that I have the means at my disposal!"

"You're a different kind of gambler," said her mother, smiling, "you try your luck with life, not with the turf and the tables."

"If by that you mean that I'm determined to turn this white elephant of a house to some kind of good account, then I'll grant that you are right, Mama, in saying so."

"But it isn't even ours, Diana," Lady Chalfont protested. "Oh yes, I know that Sir Sidney has most graciously allowed us to continue living here, and moreover has said we may make use of any income derived from a tenancy; but I feel bound to tell you, my love, that I am convinced he only says this to humour you. I believe in his heart he is convinced that we shall never succeed in finding a tenant—and I know Mr. Dally is of the same opinion, too. After all, we have been advertising for close on eighteen months, and with what result? Only two applicants, and one of those said at once the house would not do. The other maintained a discreet silence while being shown round, if you remember, then promised to let Mr. Dally know—and that was the last we ever heard of him!"

"Well, one never knows," replied Diana, obstinately. "Perhaps I shall think of some way in which we could have a school here—or it may be that some other scheme will present itself. There must be something which could be done—"

She relapsed into thought. Her mother stitched for a while in silence, then looked up, her eyes resting wistfully on her daughter's pensive face.

"It is all so different from what I wanted for you," she said, with a break in her voice. "If we had been able to stay in London and take our place in society there, you would have made a splendid marriage by now, so pretty and lively as you are! As things are, what is to become of you, my dearest child? I often wonder—"

"Then don't waste your time in wondering, Mama! I shall do very well, believe me. I am not so poor a creature, I hope, as not to be able to shift for myself a little! You'll see, something will turn up—it always does when one is at the lowest ebb!"

Lady Chalfont passed a hand over her eyes. "You are so like your dear Papa! He never could believe that there wouldn't be better days ahead—it was one of his most endearing qualities."

Diana nodded, and crossed over to the pianoforte with the intention of playing some music. She had barely seated herself, however, when a loud double knock sounded on the front door. She jumped to her feet.

"It must be Irene and Mark," she said, "though I scarcely thought she would venture out again in this downpour. I'd better go myself, for Jemina will be busy in the kitchen at this hour."

She hurried from the room and crossed the hall to the door just as an elderly woman in grey homespun and a spotless white cap and apron emerged from the kitchen quarters. "Don't bother, Jemina, I'll go."

The woman nodded thankfully and retired. She had left a pudding at a crucial stage in the kitchen.

Diana flung wide the door and stretched out welcoming arms. But she dropped them to her sides again as her surprised glance fell, not on Mr. Mark and Miss Irene Langley as she had expected, but on a gentleman whom she had never seen before.

3

THE TENANT

AT LEAST, her first thought was that she had never seen him before; but as she stood there in surprise taking stock of him, she gradually realised that she had met him earlier in the day over at the church. He was about thirty years of age, she judged, appraising him swiftly; tall, with a lean brown face and piercing dark eyes which had stared confidently back at her on their previous meeting. They gave her look for look now, taking in the trim figure in its blue muslin gown which was not in the first style of fashion, and passing on to her delicately featured face framed by soft brown hair which was tinged with red.

He removed his hat, and the rain dripped from its brim.

"Miss Chalfont?" he asked.

Diana inclined her head and waited.

Her visitor came to the point with what, if she had been in a position to realise it, was characteristic promptness.

"I understand, ma'am, that you are seeking a tenant for this house?"

Her face changed, lit up as if the sun had suddenly broken through the grey skies which dripped incessantly alike upon the landscape and on the luckless stranger who stood at her door.

"Why yes!" she exclaimed. Oh, have you come to see it? Pray come in, sir, at once!"

In her eagerness, she extended a hand as though she would help him over the threshold. His grim mouth twitched slightly in amusement at her impulsive gesture, but he thanked her gravely as he stepped into the hall.

"I fear I'm a trifle wet, ma'am," he said, looking down at the worn carpet which was soaking up the drips from his hat and greatcoat.

"Oh, that does not signify!" she replied, quickly. "At least," she amended, feeling that perhaps this remark sounded callous, "if you care to hand me your hat and coat, I will have them dried at the kitchen fire while we are looking over the house."

With a brief word of thanks, he shrugged himself out of the greatcoat, but shook his head when she offered to take it from him.

"No point in your getting wet, ma'am. With your permission, I'll take them to the kitchen myself."

He did not wait for her permission, but forthwith strode confidently across the hall in the direction of the door leading to the domestic offices. Surprised, she hastened after him. Just as he reached the door, he halted and stood aside, waiting for her to go first. She preceded him along a short passage and pushed open a door on the right.

A fragrant smell of baking greeted their nostrils. Jemina, sleeves rolled above the elbow, round face flushed from the heat of the oven, turned a startled glance upon them.

"Whatever is it, Miss?" she began, in a petulant tone, "I'm that busy—" she broke off as she noticed the stranger. "Oh, beg pardon, Miss Diana," she went on, in a different tone, "I didn't see you had a visitor with you."

"This gentleman has called to view the house," replied her mistress, with a significant look. The Chalfonts had few secrets from their domestic staff, who had followed their fortune—or lack of it—for many years. "It's pouring with rain, and I'm afraid he's got very wet. Would you be good enough to dry this overcoat and hat by the fire while I am showing him over the house?"

Jemina began to assure her mistress that she would gladly attend to this; she knew the importance of trying to please a prospective tenant. But the stranger did not wait for her good offices. There was a clothes horse standing at one side of the kitchen range, and he draped his coat over it, perching the beaver hat on top.

"There, that will do," he said, giving the housekeeper a curt nod. "I'm obliged to you, ma'am."

Diana led the way back into the hall. "It is rather odd that Mr. Dally should not have come with you, sir. He usually does so. Neither did he advise me that you were coming. However," she continued hastily, having not the slightest wish to raise any kind of difficulty, "that is no matter. Since he is not here, I must show you round myself. But first of all, can I offer you any refreshment, Mr.—er—"

"Richmond," he replied, with a curt bow. "Christopher Richmond, at your service. No, I thank you, I require nothing. I called in at the Red Lion on my way."

"Oh, well, in that case perhaps you would like to view the house straight away?" He responded with a nod, and she continued, "Perhaps I should explain to you first of all that this is not the part of the Manor which we are offering to a tenant. My mother and myself occupy this small wing, which is quite cut off from the rest."

He nodded again, and she reflected that he was obviously a man of few words. However, if he would only accept the tenancy, he might be deaf and dumb for all she cared.

"Pray come this way, sir."

She led him down a long, gloomy passage leading off

the hall until they came to a massive oak door, which had a key hanging from a hook in the centre panel. She inserted this in a heavy, old-fashioned lock and attempted to turn it, using both hands and considerable force. In spite of her fine bone structure, she was no weakling, and he noticed that she possessed the firm wrists of a good horsewoman. Nevertheless, the lock refused to yield. He watched her unsuccessful struggles for a few moments, then stepped forward, a look of amusement in his eyes.

"If you'll allow me, Miss Chalfont—"

She stepped aside, and he turned the key in one swift movement, producing a harsh, grating protest from the lock.

"We seldom, if ever, use it—that's why it's so stiff," she explained. "This door is always kept locked, and it would ensure complete privacy for a tenant, as there's no other communicating door between the wing which we occupy and the main part of the house."

Once again he nodded, submitting the handle of the door to a strong grip. It yielded with a reluctant squeak, and they stepped out of the passage into a large, stone-flagged hall.

He stood still, looking about him. An unpleasant, musty odour of damp and disuse pervaded the place. Diana's nose started to wrinkle fastidiously, then she remembered that she must not be the one to show distaste, and quickly controlled the gesture. She need not have worried, however, for her visitor was not looking at her. He was studying the walls, grey and streaked with dirt, which showed marks where pictures had at one time been hung. The only object of note in the hall was a large open fireplace which by its very size and emptiness seemed to accentuate the chill and gloom of the atmosphere.

"The carving around the fireplace is considered to be very fine," remarked Diana, in a cheerful tone which certainly did not echo her present feelings. "Like most of this part of the Manor, it dates from the early sixteenth century. There was a mediaeval house on this site, but all that remains of it is the tower which no doubt you noticed as you came in. That won't survive this century, in all likelihood, for it's practically derelict now, and very unsafe to enter. There have been a good many alterations to the house since the sixteenth century, as I'm sure you will notice, though nothing more recent than the Dowager's Wing—that is to say, the part that we occupy." For the first time, a note of doubt crept into her voice. "Perhaps I ought just to mention that the main part of the house has not been lived in for some years, as we found the newer wing quite adequate for our needs."

The visitor reflected that so much was evident, but he merely asked quietly, "Does it smoke?"

She wrinkled her brow. "I beg your pardon?"

He gestured towards the fireplace. "The chimney."

"Oh that! I'm afraid I really don't know. We've never lit a fire there."

He was not surprised; the atmosphere suggested as much. Everything spoke of long years of neglect. His glance travelled again to the bare walls.

"What happened to the pictures?" he asked, abruptly.

"Oh, we—we disposed of most of them." A trace of embarrassment crept into her voice. "We did keep a few and transferred them to our own quarters. The rest were of little artistic merit."

He did not answer, but stood staring at the bare, discoloured walls, lost in thought.

Diana felt a pang of dismay. It was high time that they moved on to some other part of the house. It was only too evident that her prospective tenant found little to charm him here. She schooled herself to speak in a business-like tone.

"There are two well-proportioned rooms opening off the hall," she said, crossing to a door festooned in cobwebs. "This one is—or perhaps I should say was—the dining-room."

She pushed open the door, flinching as a cobweb brushed her bare arm. She thought she could detect a faint twitch of his lips, but could not be certain, as it soon vanished.

"I'm afraid it's all rather dusty," she said, apologetically. "Had I known you were coming, I would have had it seen to—but our servants don't really have time to clean this wing at all regularly."

He followed her into the room looking about him appraisingly. There was a carved oak fireplace here very similar to the one in the hall; above it stood a spotted glass overmantel supported by two plaster figures of indeterminate sex, once gilded but now grey with dust. His glance travelled up to the plaster ceiling of intricate design which was peeling badly; and then to the walls covered in what had no doubt once been a handsome green damask paper, but which now was faded, torn and streaked with dirt. The only furniture the room contained was a long dark oak dining-table, much chipped and lacking polish.

"H'm!" he remarked, noncommittally.

Diana's heart sank. "Of course," she said, hastily, "I do realise that a certain amount of work would be needed to set the house in living order. That would be allowed for in the terms, which I'm sure you will find very reasonable. No doubt you have some furniture of your own which you'll wish to bring here, sir?"

"Er—no," he replied. "Not at present."

"Oh," she said, doubtfully. "Well, of course, the house is furnished in part—but I think it will be necessary to add one or two items to make it really comfortable."

"Undoubtedly," he agreed, looking about him. "A few chairs, for example, would add much to the comfort and convenience of this room."

She glanced suspiciously at his face, but it was inscrutable. She hardly knew whether or not he was in jest. She passed quickly out of the room, and opened the door of the adjoining apartment.

"The—the library," she announced, somewhat uncertainly.

Again, a musty odour greeted his nostrils. He followed her into the room, which was lined with shelves. Most of these were empty, but one section near the fireplace contained a quantity of battered, ancient volumes and yellowing papers.

"They are mostly books of sermons, I'm afraid," she said, apologetically. "Papa and I went through the books when first we came here, and removed any which we cared for to our own parlour. However, if you should wish to set up a library, here is ample space for you to do so."

"Very true," he replied, dryly.

"There is a door leading into the garden, too," went on Diana, a quality of desperation in her tone. "And only look at this delightful window seat!"

She sat down upon the faded cushions which covered this attraction in order to demonstrate how comfortable it was. Unfortunately, she only succeeded in raising a cloud of dust.

"There is such a pretty view of the flower garden from here!" she exclaimed, suppressing a sneeze. "You should just see it when all the roses are in bloom! Of course, you can't possibly judge on a day like this."

He glanced through the window. The flower beds certainly appeared to be better kept than he would have expected from the little he had so far been privileged to see of Chesdene Manor. The lawns and paths were trim and neat, and in the borders daffodils bent their yellow heads before the rain.

"It is certainly a pleasant outlook," he agreed. "And I see that we even have some chairs in this room."

He gestured towards two ancient wing chairs which stood on either side of the fireplace, and then strolled over towards them.

"Yes, but I do not recommend—" began Diana quickly, jumping up in alarm from her window seat.

Not quite quickly enough, however, for he had already seated himself in the nearest chair. There was an ominous crack. A look of dismay spread over Diana's face, and the prospective tenant hastily started to rise. Before he could do so, the chair collapsed, and he found himself sprawling in an undignified manner on the dusty, threadbare carpet.

"Oh!" exclaimed Diana, trying hard to choke back the laughter which bubbled up in spite of her efforts to control it. "I—I do trust—you have not hurt yourself, sir?"

She started to his assistance, but he was on his feet in an instant.

"Pray do not be alarmed," he replied, in his dry manner. "I can't have done more than shatter my spine."

"Oh! I am so very sorry! I did try to warn you in time—but you were too quick for me."

He agreed heartily, and regarded the chair with a jaundiced eye.

"Your—your clothes will be dusty—would you care to—"

He waved the offer aside before she could finish. "No, thank you, that's of no account. All the same ma'am, I think perhaps—"

"You are going to say," she interrupted quickly, "that you don't think the house will suit you. But you haven't seen it all, yet—"

"If these rooms are anything to judge by, ma'am—"

"But they're not," she put in, a trifle breathlessly. "There is a handsomely proportioned drawing-room upstairs with panellings, you know, so that hasn't deteriorated—and two quite tolerable bedchambers, one with a really solid four poster—"

"I wonder?" he murmured, sardonically.

She looked at him indignantly, then realised in time how little she could afford to take offence at anything he chose to say.

"There are the usual servants' attics at the top of the house," she went on, desperately, "and plenty of stabling, should you wish to bring your horses."

"To be frank, Miss Chalfont, I doubt if I shall bring either servants or horses. I have no intention of settling here for any length of time, in fact."

Her spirits dropped again, but she rallied bravely. "Oh, well, in that case perhaps you would not mind the inconveniences so much, if it is only for a short time."

He said nothing in answer to this, but stared out of the window at the rainswept garden. If only he would say something one way or the other, she thought, tensed and anxious. It was the suspense that she found hard to bear—the quick surges of hope followed by the dull certainty that he would refuse, after all. She nerved herself to speak again.

"Would you consider taking the house—" a pleading note crept into her voice—"if we were to offer it to you on *very special terms?*"

He wanted to say that he would not take it if she offered it rent free, but for some unexpected reason the words stuck in his throat. He was a forthright enough man when he chose, and for the most part this was what he did choose. But he was by no means insensitive, whatever the impression he made on others. He saw the desperation behind the girl's bright cheerfulness, and in spite of everything, could not remain completely unmoved by it.

She saw his hesitation, and was quick to follow up her advantage.

"Pray do not decide immediately, sir. It's possible that your wife may be pleased with the house. Why don't you bring her to see it? I will keep the tenancy open for you, and you may fix a convenient date with Mr. Dally."

His lips twitched again. The girl was talking as if there might actually be a rush of applicants for the tenancy of this appalling residence! He could not but admire her persistence.

"You are very good, ma'am," he said, solemnly. "I am not married, however."

"Not married?" She regarded him reproachfully. "But—but I quite thought you must be a family man!"

"I am sorry. My appearance may have misled you—I am not in spirits today."

She looked at him sharply for a moment, then laughed.

"Oh well, perhaps it won't signify, as the two sections of the house are self-contained, and we each have our own private entrance. But I can't imagine why on earth Mr. Dally should have sent you at all, knowing you to be a single gentleman. It is not what he would like, for he is most circumspect."

"I don't doubt it, ma'am. Tell me, is there anywhere we might sit down—in tolerable security, that is," he asked, with a ghost of a smile. "There are just one or two points I would like to clear up, before we go any further."

"Why yes, but won't you wish to see the upper rooms? I think you'll find them—"

"As to that, I'm ready to take your word for them, Miss Chalfont."

"And—and you think perhaps you might consider the house?" she asked, holding her breath for his answer.

He hesitated for a moment, while she ran the now familiar gamut of hope and despair.

"I think I might," he said, at last. "I shall require the use of only a few rooms, in any event. With your permission, I should like to restore those to some kind of order. But I feel I should stress once more, ma'am, that I don't expect to remain here for long."

She gave him a radiant smile. "Oh, well, as to that, who can tell? Perhaps you'll change your mind, Mr. Richmond, after you've been here for a little while. The country hereabouts is so lovely! But come and meet my mother, and we will discuss anything you wish."

4

The Langleys Take Tea

"A *single* gentleman! My dear Lady Chalfont, will you quite like that?"

Lady Chalfont set down her teacup nervously, refusing to meet Mrs. Langley's shocked gaze.

"Well, no, perhaps—perhaps it is not quite what we would have wished," she stammered. "But Diana feels that—"

"Beggars can't be choosers," put in Diana, in a forthright tone. "Mr. Dally is satisfied with the gentleman's credentials, and we may depend upon him, you know. He has been the family lawyer since long before I was born."

"All the same," said Mark Langley, with a cautious glance at her, "the situation is—um—a trifle awkward, is it not?"

He was a pleasant looking young man in his early twenties, fair like his sister Irene, and with an air of elegance which gave no indication of his prowess as a sportsman. Hunting in the winter and cricket in the summer were his favourite pastimes. He had come down from Oxford a few years ago to find his sister and Diana Chalfont were firm friends, and he had quickly fallen under Diana's spell. But she would persist in treating him only as a brother; they were soon on Christian name terms, which only made matters worse from his point of view.

"I don't see why." Diana was a little on the defensive now. "Our wing is quite separate from the main part of the house, so there's no reason why we should so much as set eyes on one another. And he means to renovate the rooms he's to occupy, so that's surely something to the good?"

"I take it that your kinsman approves of that?"

"Why certainly! After all," she added, with a short laugh, "nothing Mr. Richmond could do to the place could possibly make it any worse than it is at present."

"It is odd, his wanting to stay here at all," remarked Mark, reflectively. "There is nothing of particular interest in this part of the country."

"Did he tell you why he wished to come here, Diana?" asked Irene Langley, with lively curiosity.

"No, all he said was that he did not mean to settle here for long. Mr. Dally gave me to understand that he had recently been discharged from one of the services, and might simply be taking Chesdene Manor until he had found a place of his own to purchase. But that's of little account," she concluded, with a shrug. "If he takes the house, perhaps others may be persuaded to follow him."

"All the same, it would have been more comfortable for you, I am sure, my dear, if he had been a family man," remarked Mrs. Langley.

"My dear ma'am, no wife would ever have consented to live in Chesdene Manor!" retorted Diana, laughing. "I wish you could have seen the faces of those who did come to look over it! I declare, I almost burst out laughing at their disgusted expressions, even though I felt nearer to weeping with vexation after they'd gone."

"That's not very likely," said Irene. "Your weeping with vexation, I mean. Of all my acquaintance, you waste the least time in vain regrets."

"So she does," agreed Mark. "Her fortitude is admirable—like so much else about her."

His blue eyes fixed themselves on Diana's face with an intense look which she found hard to meet. She lowered her gaze to the tea table, and lifted a plate of small cakes from it to offer to Mrs. Langley.

"Diana," said Irene, suddenly. "Could he have been the gentleman whom we met at the church? We saw a stranger there on that very day, now I think of it, and wondered who he could be."

Diana nodded.

"I didn't notice him particularly," went on Irene, "because I was occupied with getting rid of my umbrella. What's he like? The impression I had was of a dark-complexioned man with a rather Gothic look about him."

Diana hesitated. "Well, I don't know. Perhaps that description does fit him as well as any. There *is* a sort of brooding quality about him—but he's got a sense of humour, even if a slightly ironic one, perhaps. He had need of it—" she smiled broadly—"for he was reckless enough to sit upon one of those old chairs in the room that used to be the library! Needless to say, it simply collapsed under his weight!"

The ladies exclaimed in horror, but Mark Langley broke into a laugh. "I'd have given anything to see your face at that moment, Diana! Tell me, how did you carry it off? For I'm sure you did."

She laughed ruefully. "Then you would be wrong. I apologised humbly, of course, but I feared in my heart that all was lost. However, he took it very well, praise be, and in the end I managed to work him round to considering the tenancy."

Mark Langley's eyes lingered again on her face. He did not find it at all difficult to understand why the unknown Mr. Richmond had decided to yield to Diana's persuasions. Who could possibly refuse anything when faced by the appeal of those bright, eager eyes and that winning smile? He himself was always conscious of her charm; her every movement and gesture, the expressions which flitted across her mobile face, the varying tones of her soft but clear voice—all these were like fingers which plucked at his heart strings, so that his whole being vibrated with feeling.

His mother eyed him uneasily for a moment. She was quite aware of the effect which Diana Chalfont produced on her son, and she deplored i... there was anything against Diana personally, o... she was a charming cultured girl, and to do her j... was not deliberately trying to attract Mark. But it would be a pity for him to throw himself away on a dowerless female before he had fairly looked around at some of the more eligible young ladies who were available, if not in the immediate neighbourhood, then certainly in London. Two years or so ago there had been some talk of Mark's setting up a bachelor establishment in Town. Mrs. Langley had not been wholly in favour of the notion at that time; but recently her opinions had undergone a change. Only a few days since she had been urging her husband of the desirability of persuading Mark to undertake the scheme.

"I dare say he'll go his own road, no matter what I may say," George Langley had retorted. "But here's a change of heart, m' dear! I thought you were against throwing the boy on the town, for fear he might fall into bad company."

"Oh, that was some years since, George, and I quite realise he is a man grown now, and able to look out for himself. It cannot be good for him to be staying at home under your wing all the time."

Mr. Langley snorted. "He's at home precious little, Barbara, what with goin' off to hunt with the Pytchley, shoot with his friends in Yorkshire, and traipsing round God knows where playing cricket with Beauclerk's lot! Not to speak of Brighton and London thrown in for good measure! I tell you, I couldn't stand that kind o' pace, nowadays, so it's folly to talk of his being under my wing. But I know what it is, wife," he added, grinning at her. "You see he has his eye on the Chalfont girl, and you think a house in Town the lesser of two evils."

Mrs. Langley admitted this reluctantly.

"Don't think you need worry, m' dear," he said, consolingly. "Of course the boy admires her—think there was something wrong with him if he didn't, myself. She's a fine girl; no one hereabouts to hold a candle to her—oh, yes, of course—" as his wife started to protest—"our own little Rene, naturally, though they're very different in type and colouring. But as far as I can see Diana don't encourage Mark at all. You could hardly blame the girl if she tried to set her cap at some well-breeched chap who'd pull her out of the mess her father left her in; but it's my belief she's too proud to take that way out. And God knows," he added frankly, "what other way there can possibly be for her."

She recalled this conversation now with less satisfaction than it had brought her at the time. It was only too true that there could be no foreseeable way out for the Chalfonts than for Diana to make an advantageous marriage. How long would it be before Diana herself came to the same conclusion, and seized the opportunity that was only too patently available? She set down her teacup, and turned to her hostess with an air of finality.

"I think, my dear Lady Chalfont, we really must be going. We are to dine out this evening, so we shall not have too much time."

"Oh, but, Mama," protested Irene, quickly. "You've said nothing at all of Aunt Maria's letter, and you know very well we were to ask Lady Chalfont if Diana might come with me!"

Mrs. Langley hesitated. "Well, but when I heard the news about a tenant for the house, naturally I thought that your friend wouldn't wish—"

"Are you speaking of your Aunt Maria in London—Lady Verwood, I should say?" put in Diana, who was always impatient of obscure conversations.

Irene nodded. "Yes, that's right. She writes to ask if I would like to go and stay for a while, as she is wretchedly low since marrying off the last of my cousins, and feels the need of some youthful company. I do believe," she added, with a laugh, "that she's quite determined to find a husband for me, next! She's the most scheming old matchmaker, you know, and she must have quite got into the knack of it now that she's successfully settled three daughters! Only I don't really wish to go there on my own. It was always prodigious fun while the girls were there, but might be just a little bit tedious without them. So I wondered, Diana, if you would care to accompany me? Aunt Maria won't mind—she says I may bring a friend if I wish. Do say you'll come."

Diana hesitated, and looked at her mother.

"Indeed you should go," urged Lady Chalfont, quickly. "I think it a splendid scheme—so kind of you, Irene! I shall be perfectly content here on my own for a while. When do you mean to go, my dear?"

"Very soon, ma'am—at the end of next week, if possible. Mark has arranged to go up then, to see about establishing himself in a house there, and Mama thought he could escort me at the same time. But if that's too soon for you Diana," she finished, turning to her friend, "we may easily go later."

Mark Langley felt his mother's eye upon him, and wisely said nothing, although his expression betrayed his keen interest in Diana's decision.

"As to that," she said, thoughtfully, "our tenant is not to come here just yet, until the renovations he has set in train are completed; so sooner would suit me better than later, as I'd like to be here when he takes up occupation, to make certain that all goes smoothly. But, all the same, I don't think I can possibly leave Mama alone."

"Nonsense, my love!" said Lady Chalfont, promptly. "It will do us both good to have a change—we mustn't get too much into the way of living in each other's pockets, you know."

Diana shook her head. She had a more cogent reason for refusing Irene's invitation, which she could not very well mention in front of the present company. Although she had never yet left her mother alone since her father died, she felt that she might very well do so now. Lady Chalfont had acquired sufficient interests and friends in the neighbourhood to sustain her during her daughter's brief absence. But the lack of a suitable wardrobe to carry with her to Lady Verwood's fashionable Town house was a much more insurmountable obstacle. Whatever happened, she would not disgrace her friend by looking a dowd.

"I don't think it can be managed," she said, at last, with evident regret. "You're very good to offer——"

"Oh, pray think it over!" exclaimed Irene, in tones of deep disappointment. "Mark and I will walk round in the morning, and you can give us your answer then——it will be time enough to let my Aunt know! But please, please dearest Diana, do say yes! I shan't go if you don't, I declare I shan't!"

After their guests had left, Diana admitted to her mother the real cause of her reluctance to accept the invitation.

"Naturally, I guessed as much, my love," replied Lady Chalfont, with a sigh. "Oh dear, it is so uncomfortable a situation for you to be in, and not in the least what I had hoped for! You should be living in London still, amid a whirl of balls and parties, as I was at your age, and finding some charming, eligible young man as a husband. And if only your poor Papa had not been obliged to bring you away when you were only sixteen I am quite sure you would have made a brilliant match by now. I must not make you vain, dearest, but there's no denying you are a lovely girl!"

Diana shrugged and screwed up her mouth in disgust. "Pah, the Marriage Mart! Believe me, I don't regret that, Mama! And I really prefer to live in the country, after all. But a short visit to London would be another matter——I must confess it would make an agreeable change."

"And that's why I am quite determined you shall go," announced Lady Chalfont, firmly. "There will be an extra income shortly from our new tenant, recollect, so there is no reason at all why we should not make some outlay to equip you for this visit. We could even, my dear——" with a roguish glance at her daughter—— "think of it as an investment."

Diana reddened angrily. "Mama! I wish you will not talk so, even in jest!"

"I beg your pardon, my love. But you must marry some time, you know, and where are we to find a husband for you in the country?" asked Lady Chalfont, reasonably. "Of course, there is Mark Langley—it's plain to see that he admires you, but it's not the match I could have wished. The Langleys are of respectable birth, but they are not an old family like the Chalfonts, you know."

"Well at least they're not up to their ears in debt!" retorted Diana tartly. "But you needn't concern yourself, Mama. I don't think of Mark Langley in that way, or, indeed, of any man at present. And though I would do much to mend our fortunes, I've no intention of doing so by an advantageous marriage. When I marry—if I do at all—it shall be for love, and no other reason!"

Her mother nodded. "Quite right. Just as I did, though in those days your Papa was a most eligible young man, too, what with being heir to a baronetcy and a large fortune. But I must say in fairness that such considerations did not weigh with me, whatever my family may have thought on the matter." She sighed. "How rarely things turn out as we hope! Still, we are fortunate in many ways. Our kinsman has allowed us to remain here, and we have good neighbours in the Langleys—and as you are always saying, who knows, after all, what may turn up? But you must certainly go to London!"

5

Mr. Richmond Pays Two Calls

As soon as Mr. Richmond had made the necessary arrangements for repairs and renovations to the rooms which he was later to occupy at Chesdene Manor, he took himself off to London.

His first call on reaching Town was at Mr. Dally's chambers in Lincoln's Inn, a gloomy set of rooms on the second floor up a worn wooden staircase. His arrival in the outer office created a welcome diversion to a lad with inky fingers and a smudge on his cravat, who had been reluctantly bowed over a ledger. He looked up with interest, although the two older clerks seated on either side of him continued their work, without so much as a glance at the newcomer. The boy gave Mr. Richmond a civil 'good morning' and started to rise from his chair; but before he could do so, a figure moved forward from behind a glass partition at one side of the room, and laid a heavy hand on his shoulder, pressing him down into his seat again.

"Go on with your work, boy. I will see to this gentleman. If you'll be good enough to step this way, sir?"

Richmond followed the chief clerk into the shelter of the partition, and, accepting a seat, stated that he had an appointment at that hour with Mr. Dally.

"Just so, sir," replied the clerk, blandly. "And the precise nature of your business, if you please?"

Richmond studied the man for a moment in silence, disliking what he saw. He noted the hard line of the mouth beneath the ingratiating smile, the pinched nostrils of a sharp, inquisitive nose and the shifty yet calculating eye. Used to assessing men rapidly, he decided that Mr. Dally's chief clerk was not a man to be trusted. He might be efficient enough at keeping the junior clerks in order; but, for the rest, Richmond was confident that the fellow would miss nothing that might be turned to his own advantage, and would place loyalty to his employer a long way down his scale of values. It was perhaps as well, Richmond reflected, that his own business today with the lawyer was not of a particularly confidential nature.

Brusquely, he stated the reason for his visit.

"Ah, yes, sir, indeed," replied the clerk, washing his hands in a way that set Richmond's teeth on edge. "I will just see if Mr. Dally is free at present—if you'll be so very good, sir, as to wait just one moment."

Richmond nodded. The clerk rose from his chair and, sidling over to a door behind the desk, tapped on it in an apologetic manner. A voice called out, and he entered with the same curious sinuous movement.

After a moment, he returned to say that Mr. Dally would see the caller at once, and ushered Richmond solicitously into the room beyond, closing the door gently upon him.

Mr. Dally rose from his desk with outstretched hand to welcome his visitor. He was a thin, spare man with white hair going a little thin on top, and behind the spectacles perched well down his nose a pair of surprisingly blue eyes twinkled.

"Good day to you, sir. I have the tenancy agreement here ready drawn up for you. Pray be seated, and you may read it at your leisure. After that—if you are satisfied, of course, that the terms are such as we agreed upon—perhaps you will be good enough to sign it."

Richmond sat down and drawing the document towards him, began to scan it swiftly, his keen eyes missing nothing. After a while he nodded. Mr. Dally placed before him a pen and standish.

"One moment, if you please. I will just get Collins to witness your signature."

He went to the door and beckoned to the chief clerk, who immediately entered the room as though walking on oiled feet, and stood close beside Richmond while the latter signed his name. Richmond was far from being fanciful, but for a second he had the slight tingling in his shoulder blades of a man who knows that his back is open to the enemy's knife. It was not an unfamiliar sensation to him. He signed quickly and moved away, watching Collins carefully append his signature to the document in a thin, pointed script.

"That will be all, thank you, Collins."

The man bobbed his head and left them. "And now, Mr. Richmond, if there is anything you wish to ask me, I am at your disposal."

"No," replied Richmond. "Thank you, I think it is all perfectly clear."

Mr. Dally hesitated. "It is a—um—somewhat unusual situation, to find yourself a tenant in a house that is already occupied in part by two ladies," he said, at last. "And I do not mind admitting to you, sir, that the scheme did not altogether—um—"

He paused again.

"You didn't like it," supplied Richmond, with an ironic smile.

"Well," said Mr. Dally, pursing his lips, "there are, I must confess, obvious disadvantages."

"You need have no fear, sir. I have not the slightest intention of forcing my company on the ladies—and I believe they mean to do the same by me, so both parties should be tolerably content," answered Richmond dryly.

"I am quite satisfied of that, Mr. Richmond. Nevertheless, one cannot help feeling that public opinion may not altogether approve. However, Miss Chalfont is of a very—um—"

"Decided disposition," finished Richmond. "Yes. And impetuous, too, I think. Probably not at all an easy young lady to dissuade from a chosen course of action."

"Just so, just so."

"That I approve, sir. It matches my own disposition."

The lawyer hesitated again, as though wishing to say something else, but unable to break through a professional habit of discretion. Richmond rose and gave a curt bow.

"Well, I'll be on my way, Mr. Dally. Good day to you."

After his visitor had left, Mr. Dally resumed his seat at the desk and for several minutes sat immobile, staring thoughtfully at the parchment which lay there, a puzzled frown between the lively blue eyes. There was something about this man Richmond . . .

At length he sighed and felt in his pocket for a key. With this he unlocked the middle drawer of his desk, taking out a large bunch of keys from a partition inside. Going over to a cupboard against one wall of the room, he selected a key from the bunch and inserted it in the lock. A number of deed boxes stood upon the shelves which lined the cupboard, each one bearing a label. He reached down the one marked 'Chalfont' and carried it across to the desk.

He was just about to open this with yet another key from the bunch when a timid knock sounded on the door, and Mr. Collins peered nervously into the room.

"Begging your pardon, sir," he said, apologetically, "but there's been a slight—hum!—hitch."

"Well," replied his employer, looking round with an impatient expression on his face, "what is it, Collins? Can't you see I'm busy at the moment?"

"Yes sir, I'm sorry, sir. But the boy's just this minute come back saying he's lost the packet I sent with him over to Barlow and Grundy's. I thought, perhaps, Mr. Dally, in view of the seriousness of the matter, you'd prefer to—"

"Oh confound it!" Mr. Dally turned away from the desk and hastened towards the door. "Where in the

world do we manage to find such blithering idiots as
our junior clerks? Where is the lad? Lose a packet with
which he was entrusted, indeed! Just wait until I've finished with him, and he'll know a deal better next time!
Not that he'll get a second chance!"

He pushed his way through the door, leaving it ajar,
and thrust past Mr. Collins into the outer office.

The chief clerk edged round the door and into his
employer's room, his eyes darting towards the deed
box on the desk. He hesitated for a moment, listening
to the sounds of Mr. Dally's voice raised in sharp inter-
rogation and the junior clerk's subdued and almost
tearful replies. Then in one swift movement he reached
the desk, and gently turned the key in the lock of the
deed box. Opening the lid, he turned over the
documents with deft, practised fingers.

Suddenly, he paused, his attention riveted by one in
particular. Swiftly, his eye travelled over it, mastering
the gist of its contents. A low, almost soundless whistle
escaped him; then he thrust the document back into
place, relocked the box, and had just reached the
threshold again when Mr. Dally came striding towards
him, two spots of colour on his high cheek bones and
the light of battle in his eye.

"From his account, the muttonhead of a boy will
have dropped it in Will's Coffee House—don't ask me
what business he thought he had there. Go along with
him, Collins, and see if you can retrieve it. After that,
show him the door."

                    *   *   *

Mr. Richmond's second call was at a house in Bruton Street which was evidently maintained in the first
style of fashion. On showing his card he was admitted
by a dignified butler, and a footman in a smart green
livery conducted him to an elegant parlour on the first
floor. Here a gentleman of his own age, clad in a handsome dressing gown of red and gold brocade, was sit-

ting over a late breakfast, reading the day's edition of *The Times*.

He threw it aside on seeing his visitor, and enveloped him in a bear hug which the other man suffered for a moment, before disengaging himself, smiling.

"Kit, you old devil! What are you doing here? Od's life, I never thought to see you again in London! Sit down, man, sit down, and tell me what brings you back to England. Egad, but it's good to see you again!"

"You do yourself proud, Jack, it seems," said the other, in his quieter tones, looking around the room with a swift, penetrating glance that took in the Aubusson carpet, the delicately carved chairs with their striped satin covers, the elegant and costly ornaments, pictures and hangings.

"Oh, ay, to be sure! What need have I to deny myself a few creature comforts—or you, my lad, for that matter? We amassed enough of a fortune apiece in India to keep us eating off gold plate for the rest of our lives, eh? But let's not waste time on that. Have you breakfasted? I'll ring for some fresh supplies."

His visitor refused everything but coffee, and soon they were deep in reminiscence. But try as he would, John Chertsey could not persuade his friends to give any convincing reason for his sudden return to England.

"When the rest of us used to grumble, and say how we longed to come back home, you would always shrug up your shoulders and give us one of your sneering looks," he accused at last. "And once you told me, I recall, that you had nothing to come back for. So why this sudden change of heart?"

"A whim, merely. Perhaps I missed your company."

"Not you! You're too self-contained a character to allow yourself to miss anyone. But I've missed you, Kit, and I don't mind admitting it. Although," added Jack, laughing, "as I came home with the fixed intention of finding myself a wife, I did better to come without you—you offer too much competition!"

"Stuff!" replied Richmond, contemptuously. "You know well I'm no ladies' man."

"No. But that aloof manner of yours seems to fetch 'em, willy nilly. I dare say they see it as a challenge."

"Don't talk such rot. Well, am I to wish you joy? Have you succeeded in finding a lady to become Mrs. Chertsey?"

"Devil a bit," replied the other, with a grimace.

"And you've been here almost a twelve month," taunted Richmond, grinning. "Come, you can do better than that, Jack! I seem to remember your wooings in India were swift enough—and successful, too!"

"Oh, ay. It's different altogether when one's serious—besides, I'd forgotten how damned proper English females are!"

A thoughtful look came into Richmond's eyes. "Not all of them," he said, slowly.

"You've met one who isn't? Then for pity's sake introduce me, man! But perhaps you're thinking of a little lady-bird? That's no good to me; I mean to settle down in earnest, purchase an estate in some pleasant spot, raise a family, and become the complete English squire! I've had adventure enough, and shall choose comfort for my declining years."

"I must say you look like a man in decline, lounging over breakfast at this hour of day, and not even dressed," laughed Richmond.

Chertsey yawned and stretched himself. "Oh, well, I didn't return home until the small hours—one of these damned balls!" Richmond grimaced. "No use pulling a face, you'll get caught up in 'em too, if you stay here long enough. A rich catch like yourself won't escape the Marriage Mart, never think it!"

"I've no intention of staying long in London—a fortnight at most, I should suppose."

"And then what?"

"I'm going to stay at a place in Buckinghamshire for a while."

Chertsey's eyebrows shot up. "Oho! Is this where the improper female lives?"

"If you like to think so."

His friend recognised the reticent tone, and knew better than to pursue the subject. "Have you bought an estate there, then, Kit?"

Richmond shook his head. "Taken a tenancy, merely, while I look around."

"Then you *do* have some thoughts of settling in England after all? Gad, this is splendid news! But where are you staying in London? You must come here, Kit—there's room and to spare, and it will be like old times! I'll not take no for an answer, so don't attempt to oppose me!"

"Then I'll spare myself the trouble," replied Richmond, with a grin. "I must admit, Jack, that I should be glad of your company. And not entirely," he added, more seriously, "because there's no one else with whom I'm acquainted in London."

"That can soon be remedied—there's a score of good fellows, I can introduce you to, even get you in at some of the clubs, if you've a mind. And as for the hostesses, they'll fall over you fast enough when they discover you're a Nabob! We'll soon throw you on the Town, my boy."

"It sounds as though you've a large circle of acquaintances yourself."

"Oh, in a twelve month one can meet almost everyone who matters, providing one has the right connections," replied Chertsey, with a trace of irony. "I may have been the fool of the family, destined either for the Navy or a career overseas, but at least the name's good enough for polite society. There's nothing wrong with the rest of my family."

"Haven't the pleasure of their acquaintance, but if they're like you, they'll do."

John Chertsey recognised this modified approval as the nearest Richmond was ever likely to get to a display of the very sincere friendship which existed between the two men.

"Thanks," he answered, quietly. "And what about

yours, Kit? Do you realise that in all these years you've never yet told me anything about them?"

Richmond's expression closed up in a way familiar to the other man. It was not the first time that question had been asked.

"There's nothing to tell—they're dead, mostly."

"Have it your own way. Doubtless you'll tell me when you've a mind to. As luck will have it," he exclaimed, with a change of tone, "I've no engagements for today. Now, where shall I take you first?"

"I must collect my baggage and bring it round," replied Richmond. "After that, I'm in your hands. I've no objection to sharing your social exploits, provided that you don't ask me to do the polite to hordes of females. By the way, among your circle of acquaintances do you happen to number one by the name of Chalfont—Sir Sidney Chalfont?"

Chertsey repeated the name thoughtfully, began to shake his head, then brightened. "Oh yes, I do, though—not to say know him, but I've run across him once or twice. Not always in what you might call the best company—still, that says nothing. The best company's often devilish dull."

"I've a notion to take a look at him. D'you know where he might be found?"

Chertsey stared at his friend. "What's your interest, Kit? Oh, all right, I should know better than to ask! Well, I last met him in a gambling hell in Duke Street where I understand he goes pretty frequently. We could look in there this evening if you like, on the off-chance. Play's devilish deep in those places, though, and I know you're no gamester yourself."

"Life's enough of a gamble for me," agreed Richmond. "But it'll do no harm to rattle the bones for one evening, at any rate. Or is it faro?"

"Anything you fancy, for that matter. And pretty ladies into the bargain."

"Games of chance are cheaper in the long run," said Richmond, with a twist of his mouth.

"You may well sneer, for you're in the right of it

there." Chertsey rose and stretched himself again. "Well, I must dress. Come and choose your room, man, and then we'll see about getting your baggage fetched round. After that, I'll show you the Town. Egad, we'll set it alight between us, see if we don't!"

6

A Matter of Business

THE GAMBLING hell in Duke Street turned out to be a discreet looking establishment in no way distinguishable from its more respectable neighbours. The two men mounted the stone steps and knocked on the door, which was immediately opened by a burly individual in a dark blue livery. He stood squarely in the entrance and carefully scrutinized his visitors without speaking.

Evidently he failed to recognise either of them. He shook his head. "May I ask if you gentlemen are members of the club?" he queried, in soft tones which belied his heavy physique and watchful stare.

"I am," replied Chertsey, "and this gentleman is a friend of mine. Oh, come, man," he added, impatiently, as the porter made no move to let them pass, "you may not know my face as I don't come often, but Sir Bertram Malleson will vouch for me."

This name worked the trick, as Chertsey had known it would. Sir Bertram Malleson was to be found in the club almost every night and had enriched its coffers by several thousands over the past few months. The man nodded and stood aside, motioning to a footman within to relieve the gentlemen of their outdoor attire. This done, they were conducted up a red-carpeted staircase to a small room on the first floor, where their guide flung open the double doors to admit them.

A blaze of light greeted them, so bright that at first they stood blinking on the threshold. Two young females who had been sitting on a sofa rose and glided towards them. Chertsey cast an amused glance at the flimsy, low-cut gowns which left little to the imagination and the bold, inviting eyes. He raised an inquiring eyebrow at his friend. Richmond answered with a glare which made the females bridle indignantly before they turned to slip sinuously away again.

"A pity," remarked Chertsey, with a nostalgic sigh. "But since gaming is your pleasure tonight—"

Richmond made no reply. His glance swept swiftly over the room, which was furnished as a salon with elegant sofas and chairs covered in red damask. He gestured towards a classically moulded arch on the opposite side.

"There lies our way, I think."

They crossed the anteroom and passed through the arch into a larger room beyond. Here tables were set out under green shaded lights, and men sat playing cards. A few looked up briefly and incuriously as the newcomers strolled idly between the tables; but most were intent on their game, only pausing now and then to drain off a glass or replenish it from the bottle at their elbow.

"Serious work, seemingly," murmured Richmond, with a twist of his lips. "Tell me, d'you see our man here?"

"Devil a bit, but there's another room through there."

He gestured towards a curtained doorway, and both men began to make their way towards it. As they passed by one of the tables a florid faced man with a great break of a nose hailed Chertsey, inviting him to join the game, as a rubber had just been completed.

"Very civil of you, Malleson, but my companion's set his heart on the bones," replied Chertsey. "Allow me to present you to each other——Christopher Richmond, Sir Bertram Malleson."

Malleson rose and exchanged bows with Richmond.

"Your servant, Mr. Richmond. Some other time, perhaps?"

Richmond returned a short but courteous answer, and the two friends passed on into the last room, where dicing was in progress.

They stood idly watching for a while, then Chertsey nudged his friend.

"Over there, on your left—fellow wearing his jacket inside out for luck. That's your man."

Richmond's glance flickered momentarily in the direction indicated, then travelled round the room. Having satisfied himself that no one seemed to be paying any attention to the newcomers, he allowed himself to take a more considered look at Sir Sidney Chalfont.

The man he was watching was possibly a few years younger than himself, and had more of elegance but less of decision in his bearing. His handsome face was at present flushed with wine and his fashionably dressed brown hair, somewhat dishevelled; but his features, particularly the aquiline nose, were sufficiently like those few remaining portraits of his ancestors which had been lately seen by Richmond at Chesdene Manor. The man undoubtedly favoured the Chalfonts, there was even, Richmond reflected, the merest hint of a resemblance to Miss Diana Chalfont.

As he watched, he saw Chalfont rattle a dice box vigorously and tip the dice out on to the table with a slightly unsteady hand. Then the man made a gesture of impatience and muttered something under his breath as he pushed a pile of coins and paper money over towards his neighbour, a tubby man in his forties who received his winnings with a deprecating smile. Chalfont turned towards a hovering waiter to order a fresh bottle of wine in a raised voice that was slightly slurred.

"Not going too well," murmured Richmond. "Shall we sit down?"

* * *

The first pale, cold light of day was spreading across the sky as the last of the members left the club to take their uncertain way homewards.

Chertsey yawned widely as he and Richmond followed a group down the steps to the street. "Devilish boring," was his verdict. "What say you, Kit?"

"There must be livelier ways of getting rid of one's money," agreed his companion, absently. His eyes were fixed upon the man whom he now knew to be Sir Sidney Chalfont. Chertsey followed his gaze, and frowned.

"Damned if I know what you can find to interest you there, man! Still, I know well enough you'll not tell me unless you've a mind to, and I don't mean to ask—you'll not catch me like that nowadays. Be as mysterious as you please, devil take you."

"I mean to," replied the other, with a grin. "But it's reassuring to have your permission, all the same." Suddenly he gripped Chertsey's arm. "Who's that chap? I'll swear I've seen him before—now, where?"

A little ahead of them Sir Sidney Chalfont was walking somewhat unsteadily along the pavement. The street was still shadowy, but the light from a nearby lamp fell momentarily on the sharp features of a man who suddenly moved forward to the baronet's side.

Chalfont turned hazily, and the newcomer pressed towards him, as though he had something urgent to say. Chalfont raised his cane, aiming a blow at the man which came nowhere near its mark.

"Be off, fellow!" he shouted, in slurred accents. "Damned pickpockets! I'll have the watch on you!"

The man drew back for a moment. Richmond quickened his pace to draw level with the pair, while Chertsey kept close at his side. Hearing their footsteps, Chalfont turned in alarm, but his expression changed to one of relief as his fuddled mind registered the welcome fact that these were no street thieves, but gentlemen, who had doubtless just come out of the gaming rooms like himself, "Gentlemen," he appealed, in the same uncertain voice, "I ask your help—this villain here has just tried to set upon me—"

"No such thing, sir," protested the man, loudly, moving forward to Chalfont's side again while Richmond and Chertsey stood by watching. "I'm a respectable man, sir, and wished only to talk with you on a matter of business—"

"Business!" exclaimed Chalfont, making a feeble effort to push the man away which caused Chertsey to laugh shortly, while even Richmond's intent face relaxed into a grin.

"Who talks business at this time o' night—an' what business have I with such as you, d'ye think? Be off, or these friends of mine'll soon break your pate for you, won't ye gentlemen?"

"A pleasure," drawled Chertsey. "If necessary, of course."

"But it's not, gentlemen, I assure you," persisted the man, half turning towards them, but still trying to keep Chalfont's attention. "I only wish to speak with you, sir—something to your advantage—"

"Not now, not now," stuttered Chalfont, pushing him off and almost stumbling in the attempt. "Tomorrow at my rooms—if it's business—never do business at night—be off!"

The man drew back, seeming to accept at last that he could make no headway at present, and slunk away without a backward glance. Richmond stood staring after him for a moment, then touched Chertsey's arm.

"Come, we've nothing to do here."

Chalfont removed his hat, and sketched a shaky bow. "Much obliged to ye, gentlemen, I'm sure. Not the pleasure of y'r acquaintance—" he attempted this word twice before finally pronouncing it triumphantly— "but vastly obliged to ye both—it is two of ye, ain't it?"

"Pray don't mention it," replied Chertsey, returning the bow. "Goodnight."

They moved away, crossing the road to avoid being obliged to stroll along in the other man's company. For some time, Richmond was thoughtful.

"Egad, I'm worn to a bone!" exclaimed Chertsey, presently. "I'd a mind to take you to Tattersall's tomorrow, Kit, to look over some horseflesh. What say you?"

Richmond replied with a grunt.

"Here's enthusiasm," said Chertsey, with a grin. "But I dare say you're dog tired, too, jauntering up from the country and dicing far into the small hours, into the bargain."

Richmond shook his head. "You know me better than that. No, the thing is, it's just come to me where I've seen that fellow before. It was in the lawyer's office this morning, when I called in to sign the tenancy agreement I told you of earlier. He's the chief clerk there—name of Collins."

"Oh, I see." Chertsey waited a moment, but his friend seemed to have nothing more to say.

"Well, that bears out his story, then," he continued. "He said he wanted to see Chalfont on a matter of business, and since he's a lawyer's clerk—"

"That's what I've been puzzled over, Jack, for the past ten minutes. Chalfont isn't the only one who doesn't do business by night—ever heard of a reputable lawyer who sends a clerk to hang about a client's gaming club?"

Chertsey shot a keen glance at his companion. "Now you mention it, no. But what's it to you? What's in your mind? It don't take a soothsayer to realise you've more than a casual interest in Chalfont's affairs."

"Perhaps I have, and possibly I'll tell you about it before long," replied Richmond, absently. "But he said his business concerns something to Chalfont's advantage. Now what could that be, I wonder?"

"Damned if I know—or care," said Chertsey, with a yawn. "Since you don't choose to tell me what you know, I'm completely in the dark. But if it's a rough game, Kit," he added, "recollect that we've played them together successfully before this."

"And could do so again? I've no reason to suppose it a ploy of that nature, but I'll bear you in mind should I need an ally," Richmond promised. "And now let's home to bed, and the devil take Sir Sidney Chalfont."

7

A SHOPPING EXPEDITION

LADY VERWOOD was Mrs. Langley's sister, but the two women were as unlike as sisters often are. She had married a Tory politician of no particular distinction, but with an agreeably large fortune and a comfortable house in Grosvenor Square. Living in Town exactly suited her lively, outgoing disposition; even a few days passed in visiting her sister in Buckinghamshire would soon, in her own phrase, throw her "into a fit of the dismals". To her way of thinking, there was nothing whatever to occupy one's time agreeably in the country. She could scarcely wait to return to London and her accustomed round of balls, routs, musical parties and other gregarious pleasures. Three daughters of a similar temperament had made the Verwood household a lively one; but since the recent marriage of Hermione, the youngest and the last to go, Lady Verwood had been feeling distinctly low in spirits. She therefore welcomed Irene and her friend Diana with enthusiasm, and started talking of giving a ball for her niece almost before the two young ladies had doffed their bonnets after the journey.

"I recall your Mama perfectly," she said to Diana, "such a lovely girl! You favour her, my dear, though there is a look of the Chalfonts now and then. Your

Papa, too—he was a great favourite with everyone! It's a pity that—but there, we won't be speaking of that."

"Have you perhaps met my kinsman, Sir Sidney Chalfont, ma'am? He lives in London."

Lady Verwood hesitated for a moment. "Yes, I have met him, but am not particularly acquainted with him. He doesn't often attend balls and such like diversions, you know. He's more of a club man, as I understand."

In view of the relationship, she judged it more discreet to refrain from saying that Sir Sidney was not often invited to entertainments where the chief object was to find eligible husbands for hopeful young ladies.

Although he was a personable young man of impeccable descent and pleasing address, it was well enough known (in the way that these matters were) that he not only lacked a respectable fortune, but was rapidly getting rid of such means as he at present possessed.

"And Mark!" she went on, turning to her nephew. "How delightful to see you, too! You'll be staying here, of course, until you find somewhere suitable to settle? I shan't take no for an answer; and so I warn you!"

"You are very good, Aunt, but I had thought of putting up at an hotel," he demurred, torn between politeness and his strong inclination to be under the same roof as Diana.

"When we have all these rooms, and no one to occupy them? Nonsense, my dear boy! I shall think it prodigiously unkind of you—and so will your Uncle, too—if you deny us the pleasure of your company! And these poor girls must have someone to escort them on their outings just at first, you know—though I'll be bound they'll find escorts enough for themselves before very long! But you'll stay here—of course you will! Now pray say yes, dear boy!"

Politeness having been satisfied, Mark willingly capitulated. His heart had contracted a little at Lady Verwood's glib mention of other escorts for Diana. He was not at all sure that he had really wanted her to come to London and be plunged into the social whirl which his aunt had planned. Of course, it was wonderful to have her so near to him; but had she stayed in the country, there was less likelihood of her meeting some other man who might take her fancy. Being a generous-spirited young man he tried hard not to console himself with the thought that though she would undoubtedly gain many admirers—for who could help falling in love with Diana?—few of them would seriously entertain the thought of marriage with a penniless girl. He knew quite well how his own parents viewed the prospect of a match between Diana and himself. He disliked having to cross them, but on this point he was quite firm. It wanted only the smallest hint of encouragement from his loved one for him to declare himself at once. But even in his most optimistic moments he could never flatter himself that Diana felt any regard for him other than the calmest friendship. His one aim at present was to change her attitude, though he fully realised that it would be folly to try and hurry the process.

The next few days were spent in shopping, always a welcome activity to their hostess. Diana realised how much she had fallen behind the fashions, and felt thankful that she had allowed her mother to persuade her to spend some money on new clothes. Her first visit to Grafton House in New Bond Street was a revelation. The shop was thronged with people, and they were obliged to wait twenty minutes before they could reach the counter to be served.

"I knew we should have come earlier," complained Lady Verwood. "It's almost impossible to claim the attention of an assistant after eleven o'clock! Oh, there is Mrs. Rathbone and her youngest daughter— I must present you to them, they are very particular friends of mine."

The introductions were duly made. Miss Rathbone was a petite girl with soft brown hair, lustrous brown eyes and a rather shy, shrinking manner. In contrast, her mother was a tall, imposing woman who seemed to sweep her daughter along in her wake rather like a splendid ship with a dinghy in tow.

"How delightful for you, Maria, to have two young ladies to keep you company for a while," she remarked, smiling. "I know how you miss your own girls! And your nephew, Mr. Langley is with you, too, I think you said? But we must certainly bring the young people together, must we not? They must accompany you to Letty's coming-out ball next week—I do trust they have no prior engagement?"

"My dear Harriet, they have but just this moment arrived in Town," protested Lady Verwood. "They will be delighted to attend, I am sure; won't you, my dears?"

Diana and Irene hastened to say all that was proper.

"Of course, I cannot say if my nephew Mark will be disengaged on that day," went on Lady Verwood.

"Naturally not, but we must hope for the best. I will send the invitations round as soon as we reach home. In the meantime, you must bring them all to make the acquaintance of the rest of our family. You will not stand on ceremony with me, I know—shall we say to-morrow morning?"

This was agreed, and Mrs. Rathbone paused to consider a roll of pink muslin with a white spot pattern which an assistant had placed for her on the counter. "I think this should become you, Letty," she said, holding a fold of it beneath her daughter's chin. "She is such a little brown dab of a girl, you know. One has to choose something to give her a little animation."

Letitia Rathbone blushed, and Diana shot an indignant glance at the girl's mother.

"I only hope she will come out in more senses than one," went on that Lady, oblivious of the critical feelings of two of her audience. "I'm sure Helena and Augusta were not near so bashful at her age—she is just eighteen, you know. Of course, I think it is her height that makes her so self-conscious. The others used to tease her about it when they were in the schoolroom. I told them not to do so, time and again, but there is no checking high-spirited girls and boys when their elders are not by, is there?"

"Mama, please!" murmured Letty Rathbone in distressed tones, her brown eyes filling with tears.

"What a perfect monster of a woman!" said Diana to Irene in an angry undertone, as they finally moved down the counter to make their own purchases. "That poor child! No wonder she has a rather forlorn look!"

"Horrid," agreed Irene. "But we'd best not say anything in front of my aunt, as they are such good friends."

They chose several lengths of material for gowns and pelisses, then went on to purchase some silk stockings, though Diana exclaimed at the price of twelve shillings a pair, which she thought expensive.

"I wear cotton in the country, and they are only four shillings the pair."

"Oh yes, but that will never do in London," replied Irene. "Dearest Diana, do let me make you a present of these four pairs! I should like it above all things."

Diana was firm in refusing this kind offer, and thereafter was careful not to protest at the prices, whatever her private thoughts.

They parted from Mrs. Rathbone and her subdued little daughter with mutual expressions of goodwill, and left the shop to walk the short distance to where their carriage awaited them. When they reached it, Lady Verwood began fussing over the bestowal of their parcels, so that the girls were obliged to stand a few moments on the pavement, waiting to enter the carriage. Diana's glance drifted idly over the passers-by, then suddenly sharpened as she saw two gentlemen turn out of Bruton Street and start to walk along the pavement towards them. There was something familiar about one of the gentlemen, but for a moment she could not place him. When he and his companion were only a few paces distant, he suddenly looked up and saw her.

He touched his hat, bowed slightly, and would have passed on; but Diana took a step towards him and held out her hand.

"How do you do, Mr. Richmond? I did not think to meet you here! I heard from Mama yesterday, and she said that, judging by the noise and activity, your rooms are soon likely to be ready for you."

"I trust Lady Chalfont is not too much incommoded by the workmen," he replied, gravely.

"Oh, no, not at all," she said hastily. "I was just funning, you know."

He nodded, and after a slight hesitation, said, "May I present my friend, Mr. Chertsey? Jack, this is Miss Chalfont."

While Chertsey was acknowledging the introduction, Lady Verwood, having disposed of the parcels to her satisfaction, turned and saw the group in conversation on the pavement. Her face, at first puzzled, creased into smiles; and taking Irene by the arm, she advanced towards them.

"Why, it's Mr. Chertsey!" she exclaimed, in pleased tones. "I haven't seen you, sir, since Hermione's wedding! I collect that you are already acquainted with Miss Chalfont then? She and my niece are paying me a visit, and prodigious glad I am of the company, I can tell you, since all my girls are gone!"

Chertsey made a graceful bow. "I have but this moment had the inestimable pleasure of making Miss Chalfont's acquaintance, ma'am. Before that, I regret to say she was unknown to me." His eyes rested approvingly on Irene's pretty face. "And I fear that I haven't yet had the honour of meeting your niece."

"Oh, never fear, we shall remedy that at once! Irene, my love, this gentleman is Mr. Chertsey; and Irene, of course, is my sister Langley's daughter, from Latimer, in Buckinghamshire."

"Your servant, ma'am," Chertsey doffed his hat and smiled winningly at Irene, who gave an answering smile that showed a saucy dimple in her cheek. She did not dislike this tall, auburn-haired gentleman with the carefree air, but she looked a little askance at his grave, silent companion who was standing quietly by, watching them all intently.

"A friend of mine, lately arrived from the East,"

said Chertsey, gesturing towards Richmond. "Christopher Richmond."

Richmond bowed. When the civilities were over, Lady Verwood reluctantly prepared to break away.

"We mustn't keep the horses standing too long. But you must call on us soon, gentlemen—you know your way well enough, Mr. Chertsey, for you often visited us when my girls were at home." This was said archly. "And you will like to make the acquaintance of Irene's brother Mark. He's staying with us until he finds a place of his own."

Chertsey promised readily and stood by to assist the ladies into the coach. He released Irene's hand with evident reluctance before moving back to allow the footman to take up the steps and close the door.

"Charming!" he exclaimed, as the coach moved off. "Quite charming, don't you agree, Kit? Such melting blue eyes—such a slender figure, and hair like spun gold!"

"You can't mean the dowager," returned Richmond, with a wry smile, "and your description scarcely fits Miss Chalfont, so I collect you're talking of Miss Langley."

"You're no end of a wag, ain't you? Miss Chalfont is certainly an attractive girl, but not just in my style. I like them dimpling and soft—you know the kind of thing, my boy! By the way, where did you meet Miss Chalfont? I was surprised when she greeted you—I thought you said you'd had no time to make any acquaintance in England, so far."

"Wrong, my dear fellow. I told you about Miss Chalfont earlier."

"I'll swear you did not! Unless—wait a moment! Would she be the improper female you were speaking of?"

"You styled her so, not I," Richmond reminded him. "But yes, she is the young lady whom I met in Buckinghamshire. She's my landlady, in fact!"

8

SOMETHING TO SIR SIDNEY'S ADVANTAGE

SIR SIDNEY CHALFONT was suffering from a heavy hangover. He had arrived home in the small hours in a sadly fuddled state, and been put to bed by his manservant, Hamble, a discreet individual who never seemed put out by the vagaries of his wayward master.

Chalfont had at once sunk into a torpor-like slumber; but unfortunately the clatter of a milk seller in the street had roused him only too soon afterwards. Since then, his rest had been uneasy, and now he was feeling decidedly under the weather.

He sat up suddenly in bed, gave a heartfelt groan and relapsed once more on to the pillow. That move had been a mistake. He opened his eyes to look cautiously round the room. It was jigging about in a most unpleasant way. He groaned again, cautiously reaching up to the bell-rope to give it a delicate tug before sinking back, exhausted by the effort.

Hamble appeared, soft footed. His master opened one eye and groaned several times. The manservant nodded sympathetically.

"Have you better in a trice, sir. One moment."

He left the room, to return quickly bearing a glass which he held to his master's lips. Chalfont drank it with trembling lips, groaned again and subsided.

An hour later, however, he had recovered sufficiently to be sitting before a fire in his morning parlour, still unshaven and in his dressing-gown. Hamble came into the room, treading quietly.

"Mr. Harnby is asking to see you, Sir Sidney."

"I can see no one this morning—deny me to all callers," replied Chalfont, in a peevish tone.

The man hesitated. "I ventured to suggest, sir, that it was not a suitable moment. But Mr. Harnby was insistent—I fear it will not be easy to get rid of him."

"What do I pay you for, if not to get rid of unwanted visitors?" asked Chalfont, testily—"Tell him I've contracted the smallpox—tell him anything, only send him away and leave me in peace! Egad, my head!" He clasped it in his hands.

"Very good sir."

Hamble disappeared, and Sir Sidney heaved a deep sigh of relief. A moment later, the door was flung back with a nerve-shattering crash and a portly man with greying hair and a high complexion burst into the room.

"Ah!" the newcomer said, in satisfaction. "Just as I thought! As for the smallpox, give me leave to inform you that I had it as a child. I wonder you should think to take me in with such stuff."

He closed the door with his foot. Chalfont flinched.

"For God's sake, Ferdy, if you must force your company on me at this impossible time o' day, have the goodness to be quiet! My nerves are all to the devil."

"A few bottles too much of that pernicious stuff they sell at the club," pronounced Harnby, scornfully.

"You'll be all right." He pulled a chair up and sat down close to his unwilling host. "We've things to talk about, you and I."

Chalfont made a helpless gesture. "For God's sake—I can't talk about anything at present! Leave me alone, can't you?"

"No, I can't. There's a matter of all that cash you owe me. I want a settlement. My own affairs aren't in such a healthy state at the moment."

Chalfont emitted a sound that was almost a moan. "I've told you, I feel like death, man! Leave me be. I'll let you have something on account soon."

"How soon?"

"A month—well, perhaps two months—"

"Or maybe three or four," finished Harnby, sarcastically. "It won't do, Chalfont. And I don't want something on account soon—I want all of it this time, and as soon as may be."

"All of it?" Chalfont's voice rose to a crescendo; while his face, none too healthy a colour already, turned to a greenish shade. "You must be mad, Ferdy! Why, you're talking about a sum that's far beyond my powers to lay hands on at present, and well you know it! You can't get blood out of a stone!"

"But that's just what I mean to do, my dear Chalfont. You've led me a pretty dance one way and another, and now it's time to pay the fiddler. There was that tale you stuffed me up with about your expectations—"

"I only told you what I honestly believed myself, that all my troubles would be over if I inherited the Chesdene Estate. How was I to know that it would turn out to be nothing but a liability? My branch of the family never had anything to do with old Sir John's lot, but he was known for a very wealthy man."

"And his heir was a very extravagant one," replied Harnby, dryly.

"I knew nothing of that—dammit, I was only a schoolboy when the old man died. My family weren't concerned with their affairs, for we never thought of inheriting Chesdene Manor. They had heirs enough in the direct line, it seemed—"

"Very well," admitted Harnby, handsomely. "We will say that your error was reasonable enough, in the first place. But you've been borrowing from me steadily ever since—"

Chalfont groaned. "You sound like a damned cit, Ferdy, with all this talk of money! You know as well as anyone I've had some devilish bad luck lately, but it can't go on for ever. It ain't in the nature of things, now, is it? I shall come about soon, never fear, and then I'll see you right, word of a gentleman."

"Doubtless." Harnby's small mouth set in a hard

line. "But I can't wait for that. We must give Dame Fortune a helping hand."

"You mean cheat?" asked Chalfont, dubiously. "I doubt there's a chance for that—"

The other man shook his head. "There's not. You'd be sotted in a trice, and that would be the end of you. No, I've got an easier way in mind, one that's obviously open to a man of your looks, address and birth. I'll say this, when you ain't foxed, you're a well-looking enough chap."

"Thank ye, Ferdy." Chalfont started an ironic bow, thought better of it, and groaned again. "But I can see you're in no mood for paying me idle compliments, so what exactly have you in mind? I don't follow your drift so far."

"Why this; the only thing, my dear chap, is for you to marry an heiress."

"Splendid—capital, in fact! Marry an heiress! And who d'ye think would have me, I wonder? I'm not such an addlepate that I don't realise why I never receive invitations to the balls, routs and junketings that go on for ever in the Town! It's been spread about that I'm far from being well-breeched, as these things always are."

"That is a difficulty, I agree. Still, there must be someone—some rich widow, perhaps, up from the country. Or possibly you'd do better to go outside London—say Bath, or Tunbridge Wells—"

"Good God! And what the devil should I do with myself there, among a lot of damned invalids taking the waters?"

"Find a wealthy lady who'll be ready to take a handsome husband without looking too closely into his financial concerns," supplied Harnby, promptly. "A widow would be the very thing, and you'd be most likely to find one in the watering places, moreover."

Chalfont cursed softly for a few moments, then appeared to consider.

"I've no wish for marriage," he said, at last. "But

there may be something in what you say—if there's nothing else for it—"

"Depend on it, it's your only hope—unless we can find some suitable new arrival here. And even so, the odds are that one of the old harridans would warn her off before you'd pushed the business far enough. So which is it to be—Bath, or the Wells? I leave the choice to you."

"Damned good of you, I must say. Well, since it must be—" he broke off, as Hamble knocked on the door before putting his head round it. "Well, man, what is it? I can't be interrupted just now."

"Beg pardon, Sir Sidney, but there's a person outside asking to see you on urgent business—"

"I can't see anyone. You know that—I've told you once today already," replied Chalfont, angrily. "Clear out!"

"Yes, sir. But the person—a Mr. Collins, I think. sir—insisted that you yourself told him to call this morning. He gave me this note."

He handed a folded paper to his master, who snatched it impatiently and tore it open.

"Some damned tradesman dunning me, I'll be bound—"

He broke off, frowning as he read. The message was brief enough, but he had to go over it twice, and even then, he looked puzzled. After a moment's hesitation, he passed the note across to Harnby.

"What d'ye make of it, Ferdy?"

Harnby read the message carefully, then looked up. "I think I should see this fellow—have your man show him up."

Chalfont gave the order, and Hamble withdrew.

"What can it mean, Ferdy, d'ye reckon?"

The other man frowned. "Doesn't say much, but that's wise, very wise. 'Something it may be to your advantage to know'—hm; could be anything or nothing. Anyway, we shall soon find out. Who can tell, my boy, it may be the answer to your problems?"

Chalfont laughed harshly. "Some hopes of that!"

There was a knock, and Hamble appeared again. "Mr. Collins to see you, Sir Sidney."

9

MORNING CALLERS

THE PROMISED call on the Rathbones was duly made on the morning following the chance meeting of the two families in Grafton House. Mark did not need to be pressed to accompany his aunt and the two girls; he was always content to be anywhere in Diana's company.

They found the rest of the Rathbones very affable, although Mr. Rathbone was certainly not anything like as talkative as his wife. He was a short, spare man, and it was easy to see that Letty inherited her tiny stature from his side of the family. Her sister Augusta, who was present with her husband, was a tall and imposing blonde who favoured her mother. Soon she and Mrs. Rathbone were dominating the conversation, while Letty sat quietly by, speaking only when directly addressed. After a while, Diana changed her seat for one nearer to Letty, so that she could try and remedy this. It was heavy going at first, as Letty seemed reluctant to volunteer her own opinions on any subject; but Diana good-naturedly persisted until a chance remark about the Buckinghamshire countryside struck a spark. It seemed that Letty was very fond of the country, enjoyed riding, and had once stayed with a relative who had an estate in the Chilterns.

"It's not far from Princes Risborough. Do you know

it at all, Miss Chalfont? All beech woods—so pretty in
the spring and autumn! I would much prefer—" she
lowered her voice and glanced uneasily in her mother's
direction—"to pass the spring there, rather than here
in Town. But that is not possible, of course. I quite see
that," she added, hastily, as if fearing to have her statement challenged.

"We certainly have much in common there," replied
Diana. "I greatly prefer the country—and find it as difficult to persuade my mother of the fact as you do
yours. She feels that I must always be longing for the
diversions of town life."

Mark, who always managed never to be far from Diana's side in any assembly, now struck in with a few
observations on the same topic. Letty was so unused to
the company of personable young men other than relatives, who generally ignored her anyway, that at first
she showed signs of retreating back into her shell; but
Diana, ably seconded by Mark, refused to allow this,
and they managed between them to keep the conversation going until Letty once more recovered enough
confidence to talk freely. Mark's easy, quiet social
manner was a great help in achieving this, and soon
Diana was able to leave them to themselves, turning
her attention once more to the other members of the
party.

"What a timid little creature Miss Letitia Rathbone
is," commented Mark, on the way home. "And how
admirably you succeeded in drawing her out, Diana."

"Yes, well, you did quite a bit to help yourself. I
fancy the poor child has been used to being squashed
too often by her elders. Families have often a deal to
answer for in that way, sad to say."

"Her sister certainly doesn't suffer from the same
complaint," remarked Irene, with a laugh. "She's a
very handsome woman, Mark, don't you think?"

"Oh, well enough, if one admires that style," returned Mark, with an involuntary glance at Diana
which caused his sister's eyes to dance mischievously.

"Well, she was quite a hit before she was married, I

can tell you," put in Lady Verwood. "She and her other sister Helena were much admired—they favour their Mama, you know, and she was an acknowledged belle in her time. Little Letty seems to take after the Rathbones. I fear she'll never be quite the success her sisters were, poor child, just as Harriet says."

"As I said before," retorted Diana, before she could stop herself, "Letty might do better if her family could avoid making remarks of that kind. They are scarcely likely to give anyone confidence."

"Very true," agreed Mark. "And even though the young lady may not be as striking as her sisters, she has a quiet charm of her own."

They reached home, and had barely settled themselves in the parlour when Mr. Chertsey and Mr. Richmond were announced. Mark had been on the point of going out again, but he postponed this, remaining to help the ladies entertain the two visitors.

"I am delighted that you were so prompt in accepting my invitation to call," said Lady Verwood, as she offered them refreshment. "We have but just this moment returned from calling on the Rathbones. Do you go to their youngest daughter's come-out ball? We are all to be invited, so I hope we shall see you there."

"You will certainly see me there, ma'am," replied Chertsey. "As for Richmond, here—well, I am sure Mrs. Rathbone's hospitality will readily be extended to include him, once she knows he is my guest."

"Oh, yes, Harriet is so good! And, besides, a hostess is always glad to have an extra gentleman, you know! Do you intend to make a long stay in London, Mr. Richmond? I am thinking of giving a ball myself for the girls, and you must certainly give us the pleasure of your company."

Richmond bowed. "You are very good, ma'am, but I expect to return to Buckinghamshire in a few weeks."

"Buckinghamshire? Oh, then that is why you are acquainted with Miss Chalfont? Are you neighbours, by any chance?"

"I—" Richmond hesitated, looking towards Diana, who laughed.

"Indeed we are, Lady Verwood—very close neighbours! Mr. Richmond has taken the tenancy of a part of my own house, Chesdene Manor."

"Indeed, my dear?" said Lady Verwood, visibly surprised. "How very singular! You must tell me all about it later."

"I must confess I was surprised," remarked Chertsey, accepting a glass of madeira from Mark, "when Richmond referred yesterday to Miss Chalfont as his landlady."

"Inaccurately," corrected Diana, with a smile. "My kinsman Sir Sidney Chalfont is the owner of Chesdene Manor, not I."

"Ah, yes," sympathised Lady Verwood. "Things are awkwardly left when an estate is entailed, are they not?"

Mark struck in to change the subject, and for a while the men chatted together on various topics. They were discussing horseflesh when Jack Chertsey turned impulsively to Irene to ask if she cared at all for riding.

"Why yes." The familiar dimple appeared. "Indeed I do. I often ride at home."

"And your friend, Miss Chalfont?"

"Oh, Diana is a prodigious horsewoman—but then, she does everything well!"

"Thank you, Irene," said Diana, mockingly. "Now you have managed to give everyone a dislike of me as being one of those hateful female paragons!"

"Not at all," put in Richmond. "We shall judge for ourselves, I believe."

She threw him a doubtful glance, for he was not smiling and she did not quite know how to take the remark. Before anything more could be said, however, Chertsey was inviting them all to ride with himself and Richmond in the Park tomorrow. Irene looked towards her aunt for guidance.

"An excellent notion, if the weather holds!" approved Lady Verwood, at once. "To be sure, we have no suitable horses in our stable now that the girls are gone, but some could soon be procured. I'm sure Mark will not object to seeing to that."

Mark readily agreed; and the other two men offered at once to go round to Tattersall's with him that same day, if he wished. To young men, there is no time like the present. They had just reached a decision to set out immediately, when another visitor was announced. To everyone's surprise, it was none other than Sir Sidney Chalfont.

"How very odd," murmured Lady Verwood, as the footman departed to show the visitor into the parlour. "He hasn't been in the habit of calling on me in the past—but, of course! I dare say he's heard that you're in Town, Diana, my dear, and felt he ought to come and pay his respects. Very proper, I'm sure."

There was no time for further speculation, as Sir Sidney entered the room at that moment. He looked most presentable in a well-cut coat of claret cloth, fawn pantaloons and an elaborately tied neckcloth. As he bowed over Diana's hand, the family resemblance struck Richmond once more.

"I couldn't wait to call on you, my dear cousin," he said, smiling affably, "as soon as I learnt you were in Town. I trust you are well? But I needn't ask—such radiant looks speak for themselves."

Mark frowned heavily at this, and Diana could scarcely conceal her astonishment. Sir Sidney had paid only one visit to the Manor since inheriting the estate, and that had been a purely formal, business affair to settle how matters were to be managed for the future. He had been pleasant enough on that occasion; and they had been grateful for his willingness to allow them to keep their home, and even to agree to Diana's scheme of letting off part of the manor, if such a project proved possible. But he had shown quite clearly at that time that he had no particular interest in his kins-women, and felt absolutely no responsibility for their welfare beyond allowing them to occupy a house which he did not want to live in himself. There had certainly been none of the flattering attention which he now seemed determined to lavish on Diana. She could scarcely credit the change in his manner. Presentations were made and he was generally affable, but it became increasingly obvious that she was his first object.

"Now that you are here, Cousin Diana, I trust we may become a little better acquainted. Affairs of business have so far prevented me from paying you and your Mama the attention I would have wished, but I hope to remedy that for the future. You must allow me to take you about London—show you some of the sights. If you should chance to be free tomorrow, I would be most happy—"

Diana shook her head. "It is kind of you, sir, but I fear I have but this moment promised to go riding tomorrow with my friends and these two gentlemen."

He frowned, thought better of it, then sighed and gave her a humorous look of resignation. "A thousand pities, Cousin! But I fear I must beg you to spare me just a few moments of your time at your earliest convenience—it's about this tenancy business, y'know."

"But that's all settled, surely?" asked Diana, in sudden alarm. "I understood from Mr. Dally that you had already signed the agreement—"

"Yes, yes, of course. If *you* are satisfied, my dear cousin, you may be sure *I* shall not quibble. But in some sort I am responsible for you and your good Mama—" he broke off, looking round the company apologetically—"but these are tedious matters, which can be of no possible interest to anyone present. May I call on you later today, or tomorrow, say, when you will be at leisure to attend to them?"

Diana reluctantly agreed, and named that same afternoon. Her heart was heavy with foreboding, yet she was unable to think of anything Sir Sidney could do to invalidate the tenancy now that he had put his signature to it. It had been properly drawn up by the lawyer, and was to run for a trial period of three months. Why should he want to interfere with the plan, when he had agreed to it so readily in the first place? She recalled her mother's opinion that Sir Sidney had agreed only because he felt the scheme was unlikely to come to anything. Perhaps now that it had, he was regretting his impulsive decision to allow Lady Chalfont and her daughter to benefit by it. Either he wanted a share of the income from the tenancy, or else he had decided to claim all of it.

Diana's indignation rose at this thought, even though she reminded herself at once that he had a perfect right to demand the income. Chesdene Manor now belonged to Sir Sidney; she and her mother lived there on sufferance. She must learn to forget that once it had been the property of her father, and her home by right.

She looked up to find Mr. Richmond studying her with an intent expression, and wondered how much of her thoughts must have shown in her face.

"Splendid," replied Sir Sidney. "I will do myself the honour of calling on you at that time. By the way, Cousin Diana, dashed if I can remember the name of this man—this tenant fellow, I mean. What was it, again?"

"Mr. Richmond," said Diana, in a subdued voice. "This—this is the gentleman, cousin."

She indicated Richmond, who was standing silently by.

"The—the devil it is!" stuttered Chalfont, groping for his quizzing glass. Having found it, he lifted it to survey the other man in a frankly curious stare. Richmond returned the look levelly, then gave a curt bow. Sir Sidney dropped the glass and turned away.

"Oh well, must be off now," he mumbled. "Your servant, Lady Verwood—Miss Langley—gentlemen." He sketched a series of bows. "And yours, unfailingly, Cousin Diana," he finished, giving her a meaning look. "Until this afternoon, then."

* * *

Shortly after Sir Sidney's departure, Mark and the other two men left for their intended visit to Tattersall's. The ladies partook of a solitary luncheon, so that Lady

Verwood was able to satisfy her curiosity about the tenancy of Chesdene Manor. It struck her as being a very odd arrangement.

"Not that I've any wish to pry, my dear," she told Diana, hastily, "and if you had rather not tell me about it, don't think for a moment I shall be offended in the slightest by your saying so. Irene will tell you that I never take a huff over being asked to mind my own concerns, for I am an inquisitive soul, I know! But I never repeat anything I am asked to keep confidential, I do assure you—and I know Irene will bear me out in that, too. Won't you, my dear?"

Irene readily agreed, knowing that although her aunt was interested in the affairs of those around her, she was by no means a gossip. But Diana needed no such reassurance.

Candid by nature herself, she never saw any point in making a mystery of matters where there was no cause for shame; and she certainly felt none in the present instance. She explained her situation while Lady Verwood listened intently, now and then interpolating a question.

"Very sensible, my dear," she approved, at the end. "Of course, it may not be quite a *usual* thing to do— you and your Mama living alone, that is, on the same premises, and this Mr. Richmond being a single gentleman. Perhaps that is what your kinsman means to object to—for I think from his attitude he does mean to raise some sort of objection, do not you!"

"But why now?" demanded Diana, with a puzzled frown. "The family lawyer must have put all the particulars before him when the agreement was drawn up, and if he did not object then, why should he do so later?"

Neither Lady Verwood nor Irene could find any satisfactory answer to this. Diana did not confide to them her own opinion; the only course was to wait and see.

She received Sir Sidney somewhat coldly when he called in the afternoon, but her manner seemed not to affect his determined gallantry. She found this so little to her taste that she herself introduced the subject of their interview.

"I believe, sir, you wished to discuss the tenancy," she reminded him.

"Oh, ah, yes," he said, slightly put out of his stride. "Well, among other things, you know, I must confess I used that as an excuse to see you at once, for there was no telling how long you might keep me waiting otherwise, since you were so hedged about with admirers."

"You flatter me, cousin. But do you mean to say that you did not really want to talk about the tenancy at all?" she asked, relief creeping over her.

"Oh to the devil with the—" he began, impatiently, then checked. "I beg your pardon. Well, matter of fact, I've been making some inquiries about this fellow Richmond since this morning—bit of a mystery chap, by what I can manage to glean, and that's precious little. Fellow's a Nabob, you know, like that friend of his—whatisname—Chertsey."

Diana wrinkled her brow. "Nabob?"

"Usual moniker for a chap who's been out East, with the East India Company, or some such, and made a tidy pile. Shouldn't wonder if he's devilish rich, lucky beggar," he added, enviously.

"But surely that can be no objection? I should have thought it better to take a rich tenant than an impoverished one."

"Thing is, we don't know who he is, do we?" asked Sir Sidney, in a reasonable tone. "Dally knows nothing of his family—nor anyone else that I can discover. Might be no end of a bounder, for all we know. He's not married, either—so far as we know."

"I can't see that it matters who he is," replied Diana, stubbornly. "In any case, surely it's too late for you to object now? I feel I must remind you, Sir Sidney, that there was ample time for you to have raised these objections before the agreement was signed."

"Why so formal, dear lady? Call me cousin—or Sidney, if you wish; we are kin, after all. Yes, well, the fact is I didn't go too closely into the matter at that time—wished to please you, you know, and, anyway, the lawyer seemed satisfied. Just signed the deed, told Dally to get on with it, and left it at that."

"Then why have you changed your mind?" demanded Diana impatiently.

"Hadn't met the fellow then. Seeing him this morning, in your company, I had misgivings. Bit of a sinister looking chap, I thought, and watching you a deal too closely for my liking. Shouldn't wonder," added Sir Sidney, darkly, "if he didn't start pestering you with attentions when you're back at Chesdene. Awkward, cousin, at such close quarters—deuced awkward."

A tinge of red crept into Diana's cheeks. "I myself have seen no signs of anything of that kind," she said, coldly. "And if I had, I hope I am able to depress unwelcome pretensions—from any source."

"Oh, quite so, quite so," he reassured her hastily. "You're up to snuff all right, not a doubt of that! But you may not realise what a very attractive female you are, cos—no other in London to hold a candle to you. I'll swear! And a fellow like that, bit of a bounder, no family—seeing you every day at such close quarters—"

"You know perfectly well, sir," cut in Diana, angrily, "that the arrangements at the Manor will *not* result in Mr. Richmond seeing me every day. Far from it—it's doubtful if our paths will ever cross. I should scarcely have considered admitting a tenant there had things been otherwise."

"Very true, what you say is very true. But don't be vexed, Cousin Diana—I'm only acting out of consideration for you. Indeed, I would do a great deal to ensure your happiness," he assured her, looking into her eyes with an earnestness that made her turn away quickly. "You've no notion, my dear—at least, you haven't yet. Hope to remedy that before long."

He paused for a moment as though about to say more, but unsure of himself. She gave him no encouragement to continue, but said quickly, "So you will allow matters to remain as they are for the present?"

He nodded. "To please you, yes. Besides, not much

I can do now, unless—" he pondered a moment, then snapped his fingers in triumph. "I have it! I'll come down and stay myself—a capital notion! Then I can keep an eye on this tenant."

Something of the dismay Diana felt must have shown in her face, for he added, hastily, "Not to put you and Lady Chalfont to any trouble, of course. Put up at the nearest inn—might bring a friend with me. Name of Harnby, devilish good sort of fellow—don't think you've met, but you'll like him, I assure you."

Diana felt some doubt of this, but was obliged to return a civil answer.

"That's settled then," concluded Chalfont, in satisfied tones.

"And you don't intend to—to go back on the arrangement?"

He laughed. "Don't know that I could—not at this stage. Besides, this fellow Richmond's carrying out some repairs to his quarters at the Manor, as I understand from Dally. Well, no harm in that, is there? All the less for me to set in order, eventually. And the income will be useful, too—though I'm not going back on my word about that," he added, leaning forward to give her hand a reassuring pat. "That's entirely at your disposal, my dear cousin."

"You are very good," Diana murmured, removing her hand. "Can I offer you some refreshment? We usually take tea about this time, and I'm sure Lady Verwood would be pleased to have you join us."

As she had hoped, he did not seem disposed to stay and take tea with the two other ladies.

"Forgive me—another appointment, Cousin Diana. But won't you change your mind about riding with me in the morning? Do now—I should like it excessively, I assure you!"

But Diana was firm in keeping to her prior engagement and to her great relief, he finally took his leave.

10

Riding in the Park

It was one of those April mornings that give promise of a balmy spring, and Diana's heart lifted as she mounted one of the horses which awaited them in the stableyard.

"You're sure this one will suit you?" asked Mark anxiously, as he assisted her. "Irene's is quieter, but then you're a much better rider than she is, and I feared to incur your displeasure by bringing you what you would term a slug."

She turned a laughing face down towards him. "Incur my displeasure? Am I such an ogre?"

"On the contrary: you are the most wonderful person I know," he replied quietly, giving her an intense look.

She tried to take this lightly, smiling in a vague way and looking quickly away from him; but she was embarrassed, and this feeling increased when she saw that Richmond, who was waiting close by ready to mount his horse, had undoubtedly heard what was said. She felt a moment's annoyance with both men. Why should Mark continue to hang about her like a lovesick schoolboy when she had never given him the smallest encouragement? And why should Mr. Richmond watch her all the time with that grave, intent look? At any rate, she consoled herself, it was certainly not a look of admiration. What had Sir Sidney said yesterday—sinister? Well, perhaps the man was, a little.

Once they were all mounted, they took the road to

the Park, amongst carriages, pedestrians and other riders. Irene and Diana had started off side by side, with Mark close behind and Richmond and Chertsey in the rear; but in negotiating the traffic, Chertsey somehow managed to advance so that he was at Irene's side, while Diana dropped back, riding just a little way ahead of the other two men. When they reached the gates, Irene and Chertsey passed through together, laughing and chatting. Diana was just about to follow, when a small dog which was being led into the Park by its owner, suddenly turned and began yapping at her horse.

Resenting this unprovoked attack, the horse shied violently.

Diana had been sitting in a relaxed attitude, with a fairly slack rein. She was caught unawares, and felt herself slipping. Only for a moment, however; she made a quick recovery, and at once set about dealing expertly with the situation. She had heard the quickened beat of hoofs from behind her as soon as the dog began barking; now a firm brown hand came down on her rein, helping her to regain control.

Almost at the same moment, she was conscious of Mark on her other side, also about to help.

"There's no need," she flung at him, as she patted the animal reassuringly. "You know very well I can manage a horse by myself."

The animal was quite steady by now, and she turned a brief, affronted glare at Richmond. "Thank you," she said coldly.

"I see I've earned your gratitude," he returned, with a dry smile. "But you must pardon me—one can never be sure, with females."

"Sure of what?" she demanded unsmiling.

He shrugged. "Of anything, one might almost say."

"So you don't rate us very highly?"

"Don't I?" His eyes looked into hers with a flicker of amusement. "I haven't really considered the matter."

"Hardly worth your time, I suppose," she retorted.

Then turning to Mark, "But *you* certainly ought to know better than to dash to my rescue!"

"Well yes, in general—but you were taken by surprise, and I could not risk your being thrown on to the pavement! That wretched dog should have its neck wrung—whatever ailed the beast?"

Richmond had gone on ahead to join the others. Mark's eyes followed him resentfully.

"He wasn't very civil, was he?"

Diana laughed. "Oh, I don't know! I wasn't very civil to him, come to that. But I do so dislike to be cosseted—I am quite unused to it."

"I know you are, and if I had my way—"

She guessed what was coming, and interrupted him quickly.

"Look, the others are cantering along the track—let's join them, shall we?"

She urged her horse forward, and he followed.

They continued in this order for some distance, until Irene and Chertsey slowed their horses to a walk and all five riders came together again. It was then that Irene heard her name spoken, and saw that an open carriage had pulled up on the road which ran beside the track. Two ladies were sitting in the carriage; she recognised Mrs. Rathbone and her youngest daughter.

"A delightful morning, is it not?" said Mrs. Rathbone. "How very wise of you two young ladies to take advantage of it—one never knows at this season how long mild weather will last." She nodded to Mark, who bowed and touched his hat; then turned to Chertsey, who at once begged leave to present his friend, Christopher Richmond. After graciously acknowledging this introduction, Mrs. Rathbone gestured towards Letty, who beyond making nervous little bows in the direction of the riders, had so far said nothing. "This is my youngest daughter, Letitia, Mr. Richmond. The other gentlemen you already know, Letty, so there is no need to sit there so mumchance. I declare she is the shyest girl in the world!"

"How much nicer than being such a sad rattle as I

am," remarked Diana, moving closer to the carriage, so that she could talk to Letitia, whose face was burning. "But why aren't you on horseback, Miss Rathbone? You told me yesterday how fond you were of riding."

Letty stammered something about not having anyone to ride with at present, unless she came out with a groom. "My sister Augusta doesn't care for riding, and Helena is—not able just now—"

"Breeding," explained Mrs. Rathbone. "October—the first child. Naturally, we're all delighted."

"Why yes, you must be. But your daughter must ride with us—should you like to, Miss Rathbone?"

"Oh, yes, I should like it of all things!" exclaimed Letty, with more animation than she had so far shown. "May I, Mama?"

"It is vastly obliging of Miss Chalfont to ask you, and you would do well to thank her," Mrs. Rathbone reminded her reprovingly. "Why, yes, I can see no objection to the scheme—that is, if you won't find it tedious, Miss Chalfont. But the child really can manage a horse quite well—it is one of her few accomplishments."

"I'm sure she has a great many more than even her parents suspect," replied Diana, in a light tone, suppressing the annoyance which she felt at Mrs. Rathbone's tactless handling of her sensitive daughter. "A prophet is without honour in his own country, so they say; and in my experience, families rarely appreciate the talent hidden in their midst."

"Talent!" explained Mrs. Rathbone, with a laugh. "Oh, well! But I see you have a kind heart, Miss Chalfont, so I shall say no more. I shall be very glad for Letty to ride out with you and Miss Langley."

"Then why not tomorrow morning, if you are disengaged?" asked Diana, turning to Letty.

"Oh, yes—thank you so much, Miss Chalfont—no, I have no engagement—I would be so happy—" She was too excited to be more coherent.

Mark, who had moved his horse to stand beside Diana's, now said that he would do himself the honour of calling for Miss Rathbone on the following morning to escort her to his Aunt's house. She blushed again, this time with pleasure, and shyly thanked him.

"That's a capital notion," said Diana, approvingly. "We shall look forward to seeing you, then."

"How like you!" said Mark impulsively to Diana, as the carriage drove off. "Always so thoughtful for others."

"Nonsense!" retorted Diana. "Who could resist being kind to a gentle little creature like that? Especially as her own family seem determined to do all they can to wound her feelings at every turn."

"As you remarked yourself, ma'am," put in Richmond, quietly, "that is the way of families. More cruelties are perpetrated in the bosom of the family than ever existed in the mediaeval torture chamber."

They all looked at him curiously. The impression gained of him so far was that he was a man of few words. When he did speak, his tone was usually ironic; this time, he sounded completely serious. Even Jack Chertsey, who knew him much better than the others, was taken by surprise.

"What a fellow you are for saying odd things!" remarked Chertsey, with an uneasy laugh. "I may as well warn you ladies that he only does it to create an impression. I advise you to take no notice of him, otherwise he'll become quite puffed up with his own consequence."

Richmond bowed. "Charming! And you are not even related to me, Jack, so you can't produce that excuse."

"Oh, have done, will you? I suggest we trot the horses, for they're tired of standing—unless the ladies have had sufficient exercise for one morning, and would prefer to return home?"

Both girls exclaimed against this, and the party rode on again.

As before, Chertsey contrived to ride alongside Irene. From time to time he glanced admiringly at her face, prettily flushed with the fresh air and exercise, and framed by golden curls which occasionally strayed across her cheek, so that she was obliged to toss her head every now and then to keep them in order.

"May we be allowed to join your party tomorrow?" he asked. "We should count it a very great favour, I assure you."

She turned a smile upon him that was at once enchanting and yet completely artless.

"Oh yes, of course—that is, I suppose we ought to consult Diana. It was she who asked Miss Rathbone to ride with us, and perhaps she may feel that a small party would be best, as Miss Rathbone is so shy."

"By all means let's do so." He placed a hand on her rein. "Let's wait a little until they catch up with us."

They turned to await the others, then saw that they had also halted on the track a short distance away, and were in conversation with two gentlemen on horseback.

Chertsey stared for a moment before recognising the newcomers. "It's Chalfont and that friend of his, Harnby," he said, in a disparaging tone.

"Do you think we should join them?" asked Irene, uncertainly.

He gave her a mischievous look. "I've precious little inclination, ma'am. I'm well satisfied with my present company."

She acknowledged the compliment with a smile, but shook her head. "Perhaps we might wait a little, and see if they mean to go; otherwise I think I ought to go back to Diana. It isn't comfortable for one lady to be in company with four gentlemen, only one of whom she knows at all well."

"From what I've seen of Miss Chalfont, I think it would take more than that to discompose her," he replied, laughing.

"Oh, yes—she is certainly a confident person. But all the same, I know her very well, and I can see that she is not quite at her ease," said Irene, thoughtfully, her eyes on Diana's face. "I don't know why, I must confess, if it's not for the reason I mentioned—"

Jack Chertsey's gaze also dwelt on the group. "That kinsman of Miss Chalfont's seems to be paying her very marked attentions—I thought so yesterday. Is there an alliance in the making there, do you know—or am I being indiscreet?"

Irene started. "Why no, I think not. That's to say, naturally I know nothing of Sir Sidney Chalfont's intentions, except that I've always been given to understand that he showed little or no interest in his kinswomen. He only came to see them at Chesdene Manor once, soon after he came into the inheritance, and he's never been back since. That doesn't argue any very great degree of partiality. Of course, he could have changed his mind on meeting Diana again, for she is the most attractive girl I know, besides having a host of agreeable qualities—"

"That perhaps explains why she attracts friends of a similarly pleasing disposition," put in Chertsey, transferring his gaze to her face.

She shook her head, colouring a little and keeping her eyes fixed on the group behind them. "But I understood," she went on, "that Sir Sidney is not—has not—"

"Not too plump in the pocket?" he finished, helping her out. "No, I've collected as much, too, from gossip about the town." He hesitated a moment, then continued, "And from similar sources, one hears that the late Sir Peter Chalfont managed to dispose of a considerable fortune before his death."

"Yes, it's true—Lady Chalfont and Diana have been wretchedly placed—" she paused. "But I should not speak of Diana's affairs. It's very wrong of me."

"I think, you know," he said, gently, "that these matters are fairly common knowledge. In any case, I hope you would feel that you might safely confide in me. I assure you most earnestly that I could never betray any confidence of yours—wild horses should not drag it from me."

"Thank you." Her blue eyes held a serious light as they looked momentarily into his. "I do believe it."

His own eyes darkened, and he leaned impetuously towards her. The movement caused his horse to fidget, however, and although he controlled it instantly, the mood of the moment had changed. Irene took her horse at a quiet pace towards the others, and he followed, his pulse not quite steady.

11

THE LONE WOLF

THE FINE weather persisted for more than a week, and on most mornings the same company assembled to ride in the Park. Letitia Rathbone expanded like a flower in the sun under the influence of the friendly companionship of Diana and Irene. She began to be less timid in conversation with the gentlemen of the party, particularly with Mark; and Diana noticed, not without some misgiving, that latterly Letty's shy brown eyes would light up whenever Mark came to ride beside her. It would be a splendid thing, of course, thought Diana, if Mark could be brought to transfer his affections from herself to Letty. She knew his feeling for her was only calf-love. In spite of his being two years her senior, she was the more mature; made so, no doubt, by the insecurity of her life, which had forced a more independent role upon her than was usually the lot of females in her station of life. If she were to marry at all—and she often doubted this, never yet having met a man who could stir her interest—it would certainly not be a boy like Mark. She speculated a little about what kind of man it would be: someone older than herself, someone who would accept her as an individual, not expecting her to conform too closely to polite society's notions of propriety and decorum. Immersed in her thoughts, she shook her head. If such a man did exist, and should come in her way, it was scarcely likely that he would consider marriage with a dowerless female.

"I see there's something with which you disagreed," remarked Richmond, who was riding beside her at that moment.

She started, then smiled. "Oh, I was far away in my thoughts! I often make gestures, or sometimes even laugh aloud when I'm thinking. People usually stare at me as if I'm mad."

"It's an easy habit to fall into when you're frequently alone," he agreed. "Would you care to share the thought with another lone wolf?"

"Oh, it was nothing! But is that how you think of me—a lone wolf? It's not a very usual compliment. That's to say, if you meant it as such, which I doubt."

"I fear I've not much practice in paying compliments, ma'am. No, I meant it as a statement of fact."

She was silent, and presently the grouping changed so that he was no longer beside her.

On several of these morning excursions, they had been joined by Sir Sidney and his friend Harnby. Sir Sidney had persisted in his invitations to Diana to ride with him alone, but she had evaded these, finding them yet another cause for uncertainty and a slight uneasiness. She tried to talk it over with Irene in the privacy of her bedroom.

"Have you noticed how my kinsman seeks me out since we've been here, Irene? What do you suppose he means by it?"

Irene laughed a little self-consciously. "What does any gentleman mean when he pursues a female?"

"Oh, yes, to be sure—Mr. Chertsey! Don't think I haven't noticed *that*! But that is very different—there's no reason why you two shouldn't make a match of it. That's to say," went on Diana, looking keenly at her friend, "if you share his feelings—and I think you do!"

"Oh, dear, have I made it so plain?" Irene put up her hands to her warm cheeks. "Diana, you don't think—pray, be honest with me! Have I been *un-maidenly*?" Her voice dropped on the final word.

"You, my love? Heavens no! You are a model of propriety at all times. But I do know you rather better than most, seeing what close companions we've been for almost four years."

"Well, it's true, Diana, I do—do care for him. And I think he feels the same. Oh, could I be mistaken? Could it be just a flirtation? He has a very lively disposition—I believe I shall die, dearest, if he is only trifling with me!"

At this thought, her lovely face wore such a distressed expression that Diana clasped her in warm, comforting arms. "No, no, I am certain that his attentions are serious, my love. You'll see, he'll be declaring himself before very long."

More reassurance was needed on this point, and after that nothing would do for Irene but to trace the progress of her love affair in detail from her introduction to Jack Chertsey a little over a week ago down to her parting from him after their ride that same day. Diana was a loving friend and a good listener, but even her patience was sorely tried by the wealth of trivial detail on which girls in love will all too often dwell. After listening to a great many of Mr. Chertsey's remarks to her friend, and privately reflecting how rarely the most brilliant conversation bears repetition, she managed at last to return to the subject which had served as an introduction to all this.

"But as I said before, Irene, there can be no comparison between Mr. Chertsey's attentions to you, and Sir Sidney's to me."

"Why not? Why shouldn't he admire you? I'm sure I find nothing remarkable in it at all. Indeed, I am only amazed that Mr. Chertsey should seem to prefer me to you, for you're more striking than I am, you know. One may meet girls like me any day of the week."

"Crafty puss! I know what you're at! You want me to make an inventory of all your charms, and tell you again that they're irresistible to a certain gentleman. Well, I'm not going to play," said Diana, firmly. "No, but seriously, I can't for a moment guess what Sir Sid-

ney means by it. His manner is too serious for a flirtation, and too—too—" she paused, struggling for an apt
word—"erratic—for a serious suitor. It's almost as if
he were acting a part in a play, but sometimes forgot
the lines. Yes, that's it exactly!" she finished, triumphantly.

"Then perhaps," suggested Irene, "he has realised at
last that he ought to take some interest in your welfare,
as you have neither father nor brothers, and he is the
nominal head of your family? I may tell you that
Papa is disgusted at the way he's ignored you and your
Mama ever since he inherited—never so much as calling on you in almost two years, to see if there should
be anything he could do for you. You may not be close
kin, but blood *is* thicker than water, and a man cannot
shrug off family responsibilities in that way without
earning everyone's censure."

"Pooh!" said Diana, scornfully. "We did not want
him calling on us, poking his nose into our concerns—
I'm only thankful that someone less easy-going didn't
inherit, in which case Mama and I might have found
ourselves turned out of our home and housed somewhere uncongenial to us. At least he did allow us to
stay on, and even said we might let off part of the
Manor and keep the income for ourselves. No, he has
done all that I would expect or want of him, at any
rate. Of course," she added, "had he been a wealthy
man, he might have settled a further annuity on us,
which would have been agreeable, I must confess. But
he told us straight away that he regretted anything of
the kind was quite out of his power." She paused, deep
in thought for a few moments. "Well, perhaps you are
right, Irene," she went on at last. "Perhaps he does feel
he should take a more personal interest. After all, he's
two years older now than he was when he inherited,
and time may have brought a more sober approach.
Then, again being thrown into company with me here
in London—oh, dear, I'm not sure that I'm going to
welcome this change of attitude! You know how put
out I was when he started raising objections to the

tenancy. I do trust there'll be no more of that kind of thing. He's decided to come down to Chesdene, as I told you, to keep an eye on Mr. Richmond, as he terms it—"

"He's a strange man," remarked Irene, thoughtfully.

"Who? Oh, you mean Mr. Richmond?"

Irene nodded. "I'm not sure that I altogether like him, although he is a friend of Mr. Chertsey's. He has such a sardonic way of looking at one—sometimes he almost—yes, he almost frightens me!"

"I know what you mean, though he doesn't frighten me. As he said himself this morning, he's a lone wolf—and I think it's a slightly hungry look that he carries round with him—"

"Yes, a hunger for prey!" exclaimed Irene, with a shudder. "Don't let's talk about him any more, Diana, I beg of you. You'll give me the horrors! I wish you had not taken him as your tenant."

"Unfortunately, we didn't have a long line of applicants," replied Diana, dryly. "But there's nothing amiss with the man. You're too imaginative, my dear."

12

THE BALL

"YELLOW FOR a young girl at her come-out party!" exclaimed Lady Verwood, in a shocked voice. "What an odd choice, to be sure."

"But what a wise one," replied Diana. "The conventional white would have done nothing for Letty's colouring, but in that gown she looks like some fresh spring flower."

"You've hit it exactly," agreed Mark.

His eyes turned again to where Letitia Rathbone stood beside her parents, receiving her guests. Her pale yellow gown was of fine muslin, with short puff sleeves and a softly draped skirt ending in a flounce. Her brown hair had been piled on her head in classical style and bound with yellow ribbon; while the pearl necklet and earrings which she wore kept the keynote of simplicity. She looked a little more mature, more poised than usual.

Inside, she felt the familiar flutterings of a naturally shrinking nature; but she was determined that for tonight, at least, she would not disappoint Mama. Out of the corner of her eye, she noted the whereabouts in the room of her new riding friends, and took comfort from the thought that, if things became too much for her, she could always seek refuge among them. In particular, she was conscious of Mr. Langley's presence. He was such an amiable gentleman, and so handsome—she turned her head for a moment to look at him more directly, and their eyes met across the room. He smiled, and her heart gave a sudden lurch. The next moment, she was recalled sharply to her duties by Mama, so that there was no time to reflect on the reasons for this somewhat alarming feeling.

Jack Chertsey and Richmond had already arrived, and Chertsey lost no time in leading Irene out on to the floor. Diana, looking superb in a gown of gold gauze over green, was beset by a constant stream of partners most of whom she had never set eyes on before, but who sought introductions to her through any available means. Somewhat to his chagrin, Mark could not manage to claim her for a dance at all during the early part of the evening, and wandered disconsolately into the refreshment room, where he found Richmond meditatively sampling a glass of punch.

"Can you recommend that?" he asked.

"Decidedly," replied Richmond, making a signal to the footman. "You'll try it?"

Mark nodded his thanks, and accepted a glass. "Do

you care much for this kind of thing?" he continued, gesturing towards the archway through which the ballroom could be seen.

Richmond shrugged. "Confess it's not much in my line. What about you?"

"Oh, I've no objection, if only one can find an agreeable partner," replied Mark, draining his glass. "This stuff is good—will you take another?"

Richmond shook his head, indicating his half full glass.

"There seems no lack of charming young ladies. You must be uncommon hard to please?"

"As to that, there's only one I've any desire to partner, and she seems to be constantly engaged," answered Mark in a somewhat dispirited tone.

Richmond's mouth twisted in a slight smile, but his expression was not unsympathetic. How old would this lad be—three and twenty, perhaps? Only seven years younger than himself; but it was obvious that, in terms of experience, a much wider gap divided them. Langley had gone through the normal young English gentleman's upbringing of public school and university, Richmond reflected; he himself had been reared in a very different way, thrust at an early age into an alien country, with no one to rely upon but himself. Such experiences soon turned a boy into a man. As for female company, he had always tried to avoid it. Long ago there had been one woman whom he had dearly loved but she was dead; her death was part of the bitterness that was at the core of him.

"Miss Chalfont is very much sought after tonight," he agreed.

"Do I make it so plain? But never mind—" as Richmond began some apology—"I dare say I do, and for that matter I don't care who should know it! You've been in company with us constantly for the past week, of course; and I'll be bound you're more observant than most, in spite of the fact that you seem a trifle withdrawn at times, as though you're not quite with us, so to speak."

Richmond laughed. "I fear I'm a dull dog," he confessed. "But I beg your pardon if I've intruded upon your private affairs."

"Oh, it's no matter," replied Mark, finishing his second glass. "You've seen how it is with me; no doubt you've also seen that the lady has no interest whatsoever."

"I must admit she doesn't encourage you."

"Encourage!" Mark gave an unmirthful laugh. "That's to understate the case! She repels me at every turn! What would you do, Richmond?"

"Nay, I don't know. I've no experience with females."

"No? Yet you're my senior by some years, I think?" Richmond nodded.

"Well then," went on Mark, "you must have! Come, I'll not spurn advice—I'm desperate, I don't mind telling you."

"If that's so," said Richmond setting down his glass, "then I suggest that you return to the ballroom at once, and lead some other lady into the dance."

Mark laughed again without pleasure. "I'll not succeed in making her jealous, if that's what you've in mind!"

"No such thing. I was considering the effect upon you rather than upon Miss Chalfont. At least you'll derive some small entertainment from the evening, that way."

"B'gad, you're in the right of it! I'm much obliged to you." Mark tossed off his punch, set down the glass, and turned purposefully towards the ballroom. Then he hesitated. "Are you coming?"

"Presently. I'm as well entertained here as elsewhere."

Mark nodded, and continued on his way.

A queer fish, Richmond; not precisely unsociable, but always a trifle aloof, as though he held most of himself in reserve. Not in the least like his friend Chertsey, who seemed the most open-hearted fellow. Strange how two men so totally different in character could be such close friends as these two evidently were; but of course, they had no doubt shared the kind of experiences out East which would draw men together in a bond of comradeship. Rather like a team of cricketers . . .

He skirted the dancers in the ballroom, and having reached the security of one of the alcoves, looked about him. Little Miss Rathbone was sitting beside her Mama and her elegant sister, for the moment disengaged. He made up his mind quickly. In a moment he was bowing before her and offering himself as a partner for the next dance.

Her brown eyes lit up with a soft radiance that lent added charm to her face as she shyly accepted. In a few minutes, the present dance had ended, and he was able to lead her out on to the floor.

They had little to say to each other at first, and the movements of the dance often divided them. Presently, when he took her hand to lead her down the room in a long procession which formed one of the figures, he asked her how she was enjoying the ball.

"Oh, vastly, thank you, sir," she replied, politely.

"Truly?" he insisted, smiling down at her. "You don't find it the least little bit—unnerving?"

She glanced quickly up at his face, then away again, her cheeks faintly pink.

"Sometimes," she admitted, in a low voice. "I—I am so foolish about such things, as Mama often tells me. I do wish I could be more like my sisters. They are always quite at ease in any company." She sighed.

"But they are older than you, and are married besides," Mark reminded her gently.

"Oh, do you think that makes a difference? Do you think one becomes accustomed to conversing with strangers?" she asked eagerly.

"I'm certain of it. I used to dislike it extremely myself when I was younger," said Mark, from the lofty eminence of his five years' seniority.

She glanced at him shyly again. "But surely gentlemen never feel like that, even when they are very young," she protested, mildly.

Mark laughed. "Do they not? Let me tell you I was in a rare taking at my very first ball! I would rather have faced the most demon-hearted bowler on the cricket field, than partner a young lady in the dance!"

"Truly?" She laughed, too, and he could feel her hand relax within his. "Then I'll confess something to you, Mr. Langley—when Mama has company and sends for me to the drawing-room, sometimes, I stand for an age outside the door, nerving myself to open it and step inside, among all those staring faces." She gave a little shiver. "I often wish at such times that I could be spirited away by some unseen force! I am always sure that I shall say or do something wrong, and then Mama will be vexed with me."

He gave her hand a slight, reassuring pressure. "Very natural, Miss Rathbone, I assure you. But the more you have to do such things, you know, the less terror they will hold for you; until in the end you'll feel completely at your ease."

"Oh, do you really think so?"

She turned to him with a look of mingled joy and gratitude that warmed her smile and added lustre to her soft brown eyes. She had the charm of some gentle little woodland creature, he thought suddenly; and she could be just as readily alarmed. An unaccustomed surge of protective feeling welled up in him.

"I know it," he assured her. "Already it's beginning to work, for you've been conversing quite naturally with me."

"Oh, but you are different!" she said, quickly. "I don't find it at all difficult to talk to you—you are so understanding—"

She broke off, as though conscious of having said too much, and her cheeks coloured again.

"I am glad of that," he replied, giving her a serious look. "I trust you will always honour me with your confidence."

But she was unable to meet his eyes, and fell silent.

They reached the bottom of the room and were parted for a time by the figures of the dance. When they finally came together again, they were quite close to Diana and her partner; somewhat to Mark's surprise this turned out to be Sir Sidney Chalfont.

"Do you not think Miss Chalfont looks quite the most handsome female in the room?" whispered Letty. "That greeny-gold colour becomes her vastly, and she moves so gracefully! I'm sure every gentleman in the room must be longing to dance with her."

Mark's eyes followed hers; Diana caught his look, and flashed him a warm smile. For a moment, his old feelings of jealousy revived.

"A good many of them have already done so," he said, with an edge to his tone.

"You must not mind," said Letty, quickly. "I don't think she cares about any of them—she is always the same to everyone, always warm and friendly, and—and gay."

"You, too," he remarked, dryly, looking at her with a slightly resentful expression.

She looked up, and her eyes clouded. "What do you mean? Have I vexed you—oh, pray say I have not!"

"No, no," he replied, soothingly. "If I am vexed, it is with myself. You are the second person this evening to have noticed—" he broke off, hesitated, then decided to continue—"that I have—a certain interest—in that direction."

She was confused and uncertain again. "I—I beg your pardon," she stammered. "I had no right—it was very impertinent of me—pray forgive me—"

"You impertinent?" he said, gently. "I can't imagine such a thing. And, as I said to the other person concerned, I've no particular wish to hide my interest. I care not a button who knows that I've been Miss Chalfont's admirer for several years now."

"Everyone must admire her," agreed Letty, enthusiastically. "She is so good—besides being quite dazzlingly beautiful, and such fun!"

"Yes. It is all very true. But it might as well not

be—as far as I am concerned," answered Mark, ruefully.

"Oh," said Letty, in a flat tone. "I—I am very sorry—"

"You need not be. Miss Chalfont returns to Buckinghamshire very shortly, while I shall be living in London for the future, so our paths will not cross as frequently as before. One way or another, that should resolve matters."

She was silent, and the dance came to an end. He led her back across the floor.

"May I ask—pray do not answer if you would rather not!" she burst out at last— "But who was the other person, sir?"

"The other person?" He frowned for a moment, then nodded. "Oh, yes, I see. It was Richmond, Chertsey's friend."

"Then you need not worry, I think, that your confidence will be betrayed," she assured him, with an odd little worldly-wise air. "I am sure he is a discreet gentleman, for I think he has secrets of his own to keep."

"Secrets of his own? Do you, now? What kind of secrets?"

She hesitated. "Nothing shameful, I dare say; but something which does not make him very happy, at all events."

He flashed an amused glance at her. "Upon my word, you're a prodigiously observant young lady!"

"Well, you see," she explained, quietly, "when one does not talk oneself, one tends to study other people."

"I must find out sometime what you make of me," he said, in a teasing tone.

She coloured a little. "Oh, I would not dare!"

"I must hope to persuade you, one day. And may I also hope for the honour of another dance, later on? This one has given me so much pleasure."

He could see that she was gratified by the simple compliment, and sincerely regretful when she had to tell him that she was engaged right up to supper time.

"I suppose it is too much to hope that I can be permitted to take you in to supper?" he asked. "No, I feared not. Well, then, I claim the first dance afterwards," he continued, in a masterful way, "and I shan't take no for an answer."

Letty murmured something about asking Mama. As they had now reached that lady's side, Mark made short work of this, and Mrs. Rathbone graciously consented. She had not failed to observe that her daughter seemed to be going along very pleasantly with this young man. It was too much to expect, of course, that her little brown dab of a girl should make a really brilliant match; even Helena and Augusta, with their superior looks and talents, had not managed to snare a title. Still, there could be no possible objection to Mr. Mark Langley, who had both family and fortune to commend him, besides being a personable young man of good address. The chit might think herself lucky if she found anyone only half as eligible.

Richmond had followed Mark into the ballroom after an interval, and stood leaning against a pillar in one of the alcoves, watching the dancers. At one stage, Diana passed close to him and gave him a lively smile. He responded with a slight bow; she raised mocking eyebrows, but had moved away before he could reply to this.

When the dance was over, Sir Sidney Chalfont conducted her to a chair beside some other ladies in the alcove where Richmond was standing. Out of the corner of his eye, Richmond could see that Diana was engaged in a light-hearted altercation with her late partner; he seemed reluctant to go and she to be persuading him that he must. At last he appeared to yield, made his bow, and departed in the direction of the refreshment room.

In idle curiosity, Richmond turned slightly in order to get a better view of Diana. Somewhat to his surprise, she signalled to him with her expressive eyes that he should go over to where she was sitting.

He obeyed instantly. "Can I be mistaken?" he asked,

in a voice which could not carry to the others, "or did you summon me, ma'am?"

She nodded. "I did. This is our dance."

He looked at her quizzically for a moment. "If you say so, Miss Chalfont."

She rose, and placed the tips of her gloved fingers on his arm. "Yes, I do say so," she retorted, as he guided her to a place in the set that was forming. "Oh, I'm sorry to force your hand like this, but I told Sir Sidney that I was promised to you for this dance, you see, so what else can I do?"

"Naturally I am honoured—but why me?"

"You chanced to be disengaged and close at hand, and I didn't think you would object too strongly—though you don't need to go so far as to say you are honoured."

"What else can a man say in such circumstances?" His smile was ironical.

She gave him a direct look from her frank hazel eyes. "Well, most of them would say that, no doubt, but I rather thought you might say something very much more to the purpose."

"Such as?"

"Such as that I am an encroaching female who takes too much upon herself!"

"If that suits your purpose, pray consider it said, ma'am."

"You are vastly obliging," was her mocking reply.

"So my friends tell me. Would it be too much to ask why this subterfuge—pleasant as I find it—was necessary?"

"No; the least I can do is to explain. The reason was simply that I did not choose to dance again with my kinsman."

"He treads on your toes, no doubt? And I greatly fear that I shall prove to be just as bad, for I am not at all proficient, myself."

"On the contrary, Sir Sidney is quite accomplished in the art."

"Then there's some other reason which you do not choose to tell me—no matter, I am quite content."

She hesitated. "A female should never dance with the same partner twice in succession. I'm sure you're aware of that."

"Oh yes. But I think *you* would almost always do what you chose."

She grimaced. "A fine character you give me! It seems I am a selfish monster!"

He shook his head, but was unable to say any more for a time, as the dance required them to move away from each other. She watched his progress critically, and when they came together again, said, "So much for your threat of treading on your partner's toes! I observe you manage very creditably."

"I've been well taught, but lack practice."

She looked at him curiously. "You were in the East with Mr. Chertsey, I collect? I dare say there wouldn't be much opportunity there for such things."

He smiled. "You must not run away with the notion that there is no civilised life at all in the English settlements in India, ma'am."

"Oh, no! But surely it is a hazardous existence with warring tribes and—and dangers of all kinds. I cannot imagine anyone could enjoy a ball, for instance, in such conditions."

"One learns to take pleasures as and when they can be found," he replied, with a shrug. "But I must confess I've little taste for such diversions, in any case."

"Did you like the life there?" she asked, with interest.

"Well enough."

"But you're glad to be back in England?"

"I really can't answer that, at present, I've scarcely had time to make the necessary adjustment."

"I suppose not. And getting used to our weather, for instance, must require a prodigious effort. I recall how it rained on the day you came to Chesdene! You must have found the countryside gloomy in the extreme."

"The English countryside is beautiful," he said, seriously, "in any weather. At least, it seems so to one who has been in exile for many years."

"Ah, then you do love it!" she exclaimed, in satisfaction. "You are glad to be home!"

"What is home, Miss Chalfont?" There was a harsh note in his voice. "A place where a man comes to find rest, comfort—perhaps affection? If so, I have no home."

She was nonplussed by his sudden sincerity, so much at variance with his usual manner. She realised that it might be more tactful to abandon the subject; but curiosity was one of her failings, and his statement was too great a challenge for her to ignore.

"But surely you must have *some* family—relatives, somewhere or other?"

"None to signify. No doubt there are those—" his dry manner returned— "who would say I am exceedingly fortunate. It's well known that families are a mixed blessing at best. At worst—" he ended with a shrug.

"Then what did bring you home—I should say back to England—if you have no family ties here?"

He performed his steps in silence for a moment. "Let us say that I had a commission to execute—perhaps a debt to pay."

Even Diana lacked the temerity to press him further on this issue, and they talked only of trivialities until the dance ended.

"I apologise for constraining you to partner me," she said, smiling, as they were about to separate. "It was too bad, and you took it very stoically."

He bowed. "No such thing! Could I have found the courage, I would myself have sought the honour."

She gave him a mocking look.

"You—to lack courage? That I don't credit!"

"You very well may. I am unused to feminine society, and fear to blunder almost as greatly as little Miss Rathbone does."

"You're nothing but a humbug, sir," she said,

severely. "It's as well that I'm warned, as we're to be neighbours shortly."

"Yes, you will need to beware of me."

She looked at him sharply, but his dark eyes were inscrutable, and she could not decide whether or not he spoke in jest.

13

AN OUTING TO RICHMOND

THE WEATHER continued fair and mild for the time of year. It had now become established that, whenever Lady Verwood's guests were free to do so, they should ride with Chertsey and Richmond. Jack Chertsey's interest in Irene became even more marked, but Lady Verwood saw no reason to discourage it.

It was evident that Irene liked the gentleman, and he was certainly what her parents must consider a good match. So Lady Verwood did not hesitate to further any scheme which threw the couple together; and since Mr. Richmond was staying with Mr. Chertsey, this meant that he was always invited to make one of the party. Sometimes he would excuse himself on the grounds of another engagement, but usually he accepted. Letty Rathbone was often included, too. Mark called for her whenever they were all going riding, and she was gradually becoming much more at her ease, not only with him, but with the rest of the party.

"It is truly wonderful," remarked Lady Verwood, one morning as Mark was about to set out to collect Letty, "how that quiet little schoolroom miss is coming out of her shell."

"She only wanted a little kindness and encouragement," said Diana, "As do we all, when we're in our salad days."

Jack Chertsey laughed. "You make it sound as if you're in the sere and yellow, Miss Chalfont! It can't be so very long since you left the schoolroom yourself."

"No such thing, Mr. Chertsey! I am almost one and twenty—my birthday's next month."

"Unbelievably ancient," he agreed, with a twinkle. "How you continue to keep so active is more than I can tell—eh, Kit?"

Richmond agreed, but there was no time to say more, because at that moment Sir Sidney Chalfont was announced. Both Richmond and Irene noticed the faint frown of annoyance that appeared briefly on Diana's face before he was shown into the room.

When he had greeted everyone affably, he explained that he had called in the hope of persuading his kinswoman to accompany him for a drive in his curricle over to Richmond, on the south side of the Thames.

"It's a beautiful morning, and I thought we might take a little luncheon at the Star and Garter, and stroll about a bit." He turned to Lady Verwood. "I'm sure you'll have no objection, ma'am, to placing Miss Chalfont in my care, in view of our relationship?"

Lady Verwood hastened to assure him that she would have none; but Diana cut in quickly to say that she had made a previous arrangement to ride with her friends.

"We're only waiting for Mr. Langley to arrive with Miss Rathbone before setting out at once," she said. "I am sorry, but there it is."

He was not going to accept his dismissal so easily. "Oh but surely they'll allow you to cry off, this once? I'm sure they'll manage without you—that's to say," he added, quickly, realising that this was scarcely complimentary, "there will be a sizeable party without you—two ladies and three men."

"Three to three is a more harmonious ratio," Diana

reminded him, somewhat tartly. "But I've no wish to cry off. I have quite made up my mind to ride, and I dislike above all things having to change my plans at the last minute."

"Just so, cousin. My own view exactly. And I had planned to drive out with you this morning," he said, in a jovial tone.

"Ah, but you didn't consult me before making your plans," Diana reminded him, smiling in spite of herself at his quick repartee.

"Very remiss of me, I know, but we Chalfonts are impulsive, as I don't need to tell you," he retorted, swift to follow up what he saw as an advantage. "No matter—say you'll come tomorrow? Now pray do."

Diana would have liked to plead another engagement, but lacked the audacity to do so. She was casting about in her mind for some other legitimate objection she could raise, when Lady Verwood unfortunately came to Sir Sidney's aid by remarking that there could be no reason in the world why she should not go tomorrow. After this, Diana had no alternative but to accept.

"But why don't we make up a party?" she added, in desperation at the thought of enduring hours of Sir Sidney's undiluted company.

"Mr. Langley has his curricle here, and I know his sister would like to accompany us, would you not, Irene?"

Realising that this was what her friend wished her to say, Irene instantly agreed.

"A capital notion!" seconded Chertsey, quickly. "And Kit and I will join you—if you've no objection, that is, Chalfont?"

Sir Sidney replied that of course he would be happy, but his countenance belied the words. It was Richmond who struck the first discordant note by saying that he had a previous engagement which would prevent his making one of the party.

"Put it off, my dear fellow," suggested Chertsey. "It can't be so urgent that it won't wait for one more day."

Richmond stood firm, however, and after a further demur, his friend left him alone. Kit could be devilish obstinate at times, as he knew from past experience; and anyway, there would be too many men in the party as it was. It was this thought that prompted him to suggest that Miss Rathbone might like to go along with them.

"She could go in your brother's curricle, Miss Langley, as it would be a poor thing for brother and sister to travel together. I am persuaded you would soon be at outs—so it always is," he told Irene, laughing.

"No such thing; Mark and I rarely quarrel," she protested, with an answering smile. "But if Letty does come, perhaps she would be more comfortable with Mark. She must be quite used to him by now, as he's been escorting her to and from her home every day we've gone riding together."

"Why, yes, that is very true," said Lady Verwood. "And I am sure her Mama would not have the least objection to Letty's joining your party, Sir Sidney— such a splendid notion, and we need only hope for another fine day!"

Thus Sir Sidney found himself unwillingly sponsoring an expedition instead of being able to look forward to the whole day's tête-à-tête with Diana which he had intended. He took the change in good part, however, and left them with his customary affability.

"Well, thank goodness we won't have to endure the company of Mr. Harnby, at any rate!" said Diana to Irene, as they were riding side by side in the Park. "I cannot stand that man!"

"Neither can I," admitted Irene. "I don't know what it is, quite—"

"I do! He is pompous, insincere and vulgar besides! I don't know how my kinsman comes to be in such close friendship with him, for at least Sir Sidney is a gentleman."

Irene agreed. "I've sometimes fancied that your kinsman seems a little afraid of Mr. Harnby," she continued, hesitantly. "At least, not afraid, precisely—but something very like it."

Diana frowned. "He does seem inclined to defer to him; and it can't be to his superior character, or judgment, that's certain! Possibly he owes the man some money—"

"Who owes whom some money?" asked Mark, riding up beside them.

Irene repeated what had been said. He shrugged.

"Can't say— I've not been in Town long enough to hear that kind of thing. But I'll ask Chertsey, if you like. He's alive on all suits. Come to that," he finished, giving his sister a sly look, "you could ask him yourself. You're getting to be deuced confidential together."

Irene coloured, and retorted that she would never dream of putting such an improper question.

"Oh, no! You're all propriety, when it suits you, miss!" he teased her. He turned to Diana with a different expression on his face. "But if you really want to know, Diana—"

"It's of no consequence. Just an idle thought, that's all," replied Diana, carelessly.

But even Diana's idle thoughts were of some importance to Mark; or at any rate, he still believed they were, which came to the same thing. When the opportunity came, therefore, he did put the question to Jack Chertsey, and in Richmond's hearing.

"I've heard rumours," replied Chertsey, "and it certainly wouldn't surprise me, for why else a man of Chalfont's standing should tolerate the company of such a vulgar upstart is more than I can reckon. Besides, I was warned off the man myself by a very good friend of mine when first I came on the Town. Called him a gull-snatcher—said he hung around the gaming hells looking for plump pigeons for the snaring. Mind you, I don't think it's generally known, and the fellow seems popular enough with the hard gamesters."

"Which Chalfont is?"

"Never a doubt of it! By all accounts, it's a Chalfont vice." He lowered his voice, glancing towards the three girls who were riding a little way ahead at the time. "I collect Miss Chalfont's father was pretty well rolled up when he quitted Town for Buckinghamshire, a few years before his death."

Mark gave no other answer than a brusque nod, before urging his horse to a trot so that he might join the ladies.

*   *   *

The outing to Richmond on the following day certainly started well. The weather was very kind for April; there was no wind, and the sun was quite hot. If Mark was a little disappointed at having to take Letty in his curricle instead of Diana, his gentle good manners did not allow him to betray the fact.

Indeed, after a while in Letty's company, he could not help reflecting that though she was not such a lively, entertaining girl as Diana, she was perhaps more restful. Then, too, it was rather flattering, after Diana's sisterly treatment of him, to have someone hanging upon his words as though they were pure pearls of wisdom dropped from the mouth of Solomon. As for Letty, her feelings were much less complex. She had fallen head over heels in love with this handsome young man, at her coming-out ball, and all she asked of life was to be allowed to spend every possible moment in his company. Too young and inexperienced to have cultivated any arts by which she might attempt to captivate him, she was unconsciously helping on her purpose by her very artlessness.

"How well you drive, Mr. Langley," she said, in her soft, shy voice. "I wish I could do it!"

"Do you?" he asked her, smiling. "You must permit me to teach you."

"Oh, no!" she exclaimed, hurriedly. "I'm sure I should be far too stupid at it—I should vex you."

He protested gallantly, telling her that he had taught Miss Chalfont a few years back.

"But Miss Chalfont is so clever," she said, sadly. "I'm sure she would be an excellent pupil."

A picture flashed across his mind of Diana, at much the same age as the girl at his side, handling a pair of lively high-stepping chestnuts as though she had done nothing else all her life. There had been little to teach her; she had seemed to have a way with horses from the start. She had so much confidence in herself, he thought ruefully. Could it be that she was completely self-reliant, that she needed no one to lean upon? Even if she did, he had a growing conviction that he was not the man she needed. On the other hand, Miss Letty . . .

He turned a masterful look upon her.

"And so you will be," he promised. "If your mother will allow it, I shall start teaching you tomorrow—that is," he added—tempering this high-handedness with politeness—"if you have no previous engagements to interfere with the plan."

Hastily dismissing from her mind an already overdue visit to the dressmaker, she expressed her readiness to start the lessons on the following day.

"Oh, I do hope Mama won't refuse!" she finished, looking at him with troubled eyes.

He undertook to seek her mother's permission when they returned home, and there was nothing left then to interfere with her enjoyment of the drive, the sunny April day and his company.

Irene and Chertsey were similarly deriving considerable enjoyment from the outing; Diana alone of all the party was cordially wishing herself elsewhere. One of the irritations she was called upon to suffer was Sir Sidney's erratic driving. He was far from being the accomplished whip that Mark, or even Diana herself, was; and, as he gave little of his attention to the road and far more to herself than she welcomed, she was constantly in a fidget in case he should put them in a ditch. After they had covered the first five miles, miraculously (it seemed to her) without an accident, she begged him to let her drive for a while. He resisted the idea, at first gallantly and later with more candour.

"Ladies should never drive," he pronounced. "They haven't the temperament for it."

"Indeed," replied Diana, coldly.

"Well, stands to reason, don't it? Handling the ribbons takes a cool head, and what female can claim to have——" he broke off as they rounded a bend and came upon a farm wagon plumb in the centre of the road. "Hey, you, fellow!" he shouted to the farm hand. "Move over, can't you?"

The carter appeared to be deaf, or possibly he had heard somewhere that Jack was as good as his master, for he paid no heed to this appeal. Sir Sidney's voice rose, and with it his colour.

"Damn the stupid oaf! Move over at once, I say, or I'll take my whip to you!"

Diana looked at her kinsman judicially. "Mm, yes," she commented dryly. "A cool head. I see."

"Now, don't *you* start tormenting me, cousin, while I've got this idiot to deal with!" He addressed the wagoner again, in tones which must have carried as far as the farm across the adjacent field. "You misbegotten son of a witch——!"

At this point Jack Chertsey's curricle rounded the bend and would have collided with Chalfont's stationary vehicle but for some neat wrist work on Chertsey's part.

"What now, Chalfont?" he demanded. "This isn't a good spot for holding a meeting, in my opinion! Horse shed a shoe, or something?"

"Nothing of the kind!" snapped Sir Sidney, with unabated choler. "It's this damned labourer refused to budge, but I'll deal with him, never fear!"

He started to rise from his seat.

"If you're going to do that," said Diana, sweetly, "I think I'd better have the reins."

He handed them to her with a sullen look, and sprang down from the vehicle, whip in hand. But before he could reach the carter's side, the man had pulled his cart well in to the side of the road, leaving ample room for the curricle to pass.

Sir Sidney continued to advance with upraised whip, and would no doubt have used it to some effect about the carter's shoulders; but just as he drew level with the man, he was startled by a curricle dashing past within inches of where he stood.

He turned in amazement to see that it was his own vehicle, with Diana driving. Having passed the cart, she drew to a standstill a little farther along the road, waiting for her ex-driver to catch up with her. Truth to tell, she had been sorely tempted to give him a longer run for his money, but she restrained the unworthy impulse.

No sooner had she gone past, than Chertsey's curricle swept past the cart, too; and Mark, who had just arrived on the scene, demanded to be told what was happening.

"See for yourself," shouted Chalfont, his temper not improved by being made to look a fool in front of the other two men. He decided against making a physical protest to the cause of the trouble, however; contenting himself with a string of colourful abuse which fortunately could not be heard by Letty, although Mark looked anxiously at her. Then Sir Sidney turned on his heel and strode towards his own curricle.

Having reached it, he made as if to mount into the driving seat; but Diana showed no indication of making way for him, so he was obliged to travel as a passenger for the remaining few miles of the journey. Like most people who lose their temper easily he was also very quick to recover it; soon he was complimenting Diana on her ability to manage a pair of horses, and from that tribute proceeding glibly to others which she told herself were not nearly so well deserved. In fact, he became just as tiresomely gallant as he had been on every occasion recently whenever they had met.

Once again, Diana puzzled over what he could mean by it. Allowing for the fact that young men usually felt impelled to treat nubile young ladies to a display of gallantry, more especially in fashionable circles, the fact of their relationship would surely have excused him from this particular form of civility. Neither could she believe that he had fallen seriously in love with her; there was no warmth, no depth of sincerity behind the attentions he paid her. Why he should waste his time and hers with such nonsense, she thought impatiently, was more than she could surmise. A light-hearted flirtation was something she could take part in readily enough, provided she found the gentleman reasonably attractive; she had played her fair share in that way at the Rathbones' ball. But although Sir Sidney was sufficiently good-looking and well-groomed to appeal, no doubt, to plenty of other girls, he completely failed to attract Diana. She reflected with a slight feeling of dismay that perhaps the man did not exist who could arouse in her any lasting emotional response. Perhaps she was destined to be a self-appointed old maid.

She gave no indication of what was passing in her mind, but gradually steered the conversation round to horseflesh, a subject which she guessed might keep him talking for some time, thus staving off unwanted gallantries. She succeeded so well that the topic was barely exhausted by the time they reached their destination.

The curricles were stabled at the Star and Garter and a luncheon bespoken for the party for half past one. This left more than an hour to while away, and by common consent it was decided to stroll down to the river. Diana, her arm linked through Irene's, paused first to admire the fine view from their vantage point on Richmond Hill. Wooded green meadows sloped down to the Thames, glinting in the sunlight as it curved towards the tree-clad Twickenham bank. A small island nestled in the bend of the river, slashing the silver sleeve with an inset of green; and tiny boats, diminished by distance, trailed a thin white wake around it.

"Perfect!" breathed Diana. "At least I shall have one lovely memory to take back with me to Chesdene."

"You make it sound as if you're returning tomorrow," said Irene, uneasily.

"Well, I must return soon—I think by the end of this week. I had a letter from Mama this morning, and she says the work being done for Mr. Richmond is almost finished. That means he will be returning to Chesdene himself before long, and I want to be home when he is there."

"Oh, no!" exclaimed Irene, involuntarily.

Diana looked at her quickly. "You don't want to go?" she asked, in a low tone, glancing at the others. Mark had given his arm to Letty, and they were strolling on ahead, while Chalfont and Chertsey were chatting together a little distance apart.

"Well, there's no reason why you should. I'm sure your aunt will be delighted to keep you for a while longer; and as Mark's just found a suitable house for his occupation, he'll be glad to have your advice in furnishing it."

"But I can't let you return to Chesdene alone—that would be shabby of me, indeed! Especially since you came here in the first place to oblige me."

They had not noticed that Sir Sidney and Jack Chertsey had drawn closer to them, and now Chalfont spoke. "Return to Chesdene alone—who? Do you mean you intend to do so, Cousin Diana? When?"

She was obliged to repeat what she had been saying.

"You may be easy, ma'am," said Chalfont to Irene. "I certainly shan't allow my kinswoman to travel home alone. I myself will accompany her whenever she pleases."

"But there is no need of that!" protested Diana, feeling annoyed at his proprietorial air. "A distance of thirty miles or so—barely a morning's journey! No, if you will lend me your maid to accompany me, Irene, for half a day, she can return on the stage coach. Nothing more is necessary."

Irene readily agreed to this, but Sir Sidney was so persistent in continuing to offer his escort, that Diana lost a little of her usual civility.

"Oh, very well, sir!" she exclaimed, tartly. "If you're determined to come, I can't very well stop you!"

It was obvious that Diana had endured as much of her kinsman's company as she could take at present, so Irene good-naturedly claimed his attention for herself. Ignoring Chertsey's hints and sighs, she placed her hand on the sleeve of Chalfont's coat, and turned upon him the full battery of her charming smile and dancing blue eyes.

Chertsey quickly realised what she intended, and leaving Mark to walk beside Letty, placed himself next to Diana. Both of them were especially apt at light-hearted conversation and were soon laughing and talking together, Diana's good humour quite restored. Presently he offered her his arm, for the party had turned into a steep lane sloping down to the river, and there were some rough, stony patches.

"The view which you were admiring just now," said Mark, turning his head to address Diana, "was also, I understand, admired by an American called William Byrd. It put him in mind of a view near his home in Virginia, so when he returned, he gave the name of Richmond to a town on the James River."

They all showed some interest in this, and Letty, for once finding courage to volunteer a remark, said that she believed there was also a town of Richmond in Yorkshire. Mark at once told her that he had visited it, going on to describe the tiny theatre there.

"Curious, don't you think," remarked Chertsey to Diana, "that we should have visited this place without the one man who ought to have felt especially at home here?"

They had drawn a little apart again from the others. She looked puzzled for a moment.

"The man who——? Oh, you mean, Mr. Richmond!" She laughed. "Of course—he has the same name. I suppose his family isn't from these parts, by any chance? That would be a very odd coincidence, indeed!"

"Dashed if I know," replied Chertsey. "Kit never

speaks of his family—will have it he hasn't one, though I doubt that."

Diana looked thoughtful. "Perhaps even if he has, he prefers to forget them," she said. "He did say something of the kind to me once."

Chertsey cocked a quizzical eyebrow at her. "So you two have been talking confidences together?"

"I think you'll allow that it isn't easy to talk confidences in a ballroom," she countered, in the same tone as he had used.

"Not a bit of it! I see couples contriving to do so whenever I attend one."

"And no doubt you yourself among them, sir!"

"Well—given the right company, of course, I must confess it is a temptation hard to resist."

She flashed him the smile that made her eyes dance, and that always affected Mark so powerfully.

"But naturally you try your best, do you not?"

"As to that, Miss Chalfont—"

"Don't trouble to try and humbug me, Mr. Chertsey!"

They both laughed, and Sir Sidney turned round for a moment to look at them, a frown gathering on his brow.

14

RICHMOND PURCHASES A PICTURE

WHILE HIS friends were strolling beside the Thames on this warm day in spring, Richmond was busy with his own affairs in London. One of his errands was to a shop in St. Paul's Churchyard. At almost any time of day there would be a group of people loitering outside it, peering into the window, which displayed a selection of the latest prints and caricatures. He, too, paused before entering the shop, his amused eye lighting on two prints of Gillray's displayed side by side. The first, entitled 'Harmony before Matrimony', showed a yearning suitor holding the music while his languishing love played the harp; the second had the title 'Matrimonial Harmonies', and here a yelling baby combined with his piano-playing Mama to produce a terrifying volume of sound which Papa was vainly trying to escape.

Richmond's wry smile was in evidence as he entered the shop. There was an even more impressive display of graphic art within, and in spite of his determination to keep to the matter in hand, he found his attention caught once more.

The shopkeeper waited patiently while his customer studied the prints. Such matters could not be hurried; if a customer were allowed to browse, he might purchase more than he had originally intended. On the other hand, he might well go away with only a sixpenny print, or nothing at all, like the dozens who looked their fill daily at the window display without spending a penny in his shop. No matter. He was a philosophical man, for his was a philosophical trade, one might fairly say, as it dealt in social satire.

Richmond turned firmly away from the pictures. "I have business with a Mr. Bowles," he said. "My name is Richmond."

"Ah, yes, sir, to be sure," replied the shopkeeper, going through the motions of washing his hands. "If you'll please to step this way, sir?"

He raised the counter flap to admit Richmond, and conducted him into a small room at the back of the shop.

"Gentleman to see ye, Jerry, name of Richmond, ye'll recall?"

He went away, closing the door behind him.

The man who was standing before an easel in the window looked up, flinging down his brush. He nodded casually to Richmond, and, seizing a rag, began to rub his hands on it vigorously.

"I'd ask you to sit down," he said, brusquely, "but that there isn't anywhere to sit, unless you count the floor."

Richmond's glance travelled briefly over the cluttered room. It bore evidences not only of its occupant's calling but of his absorbing interest in it—the congealing chop on a plate, the nightshirt, waistcoat and jacket lying discarded on the floor, all spoke of a man who considered eating and dressing to be secondary considerations in his life.

"I hope not to be here long enough for sitting. Did you manage to get the pictures?"

Bowles nodded. "Most of them, at any rate. But God knows what you want them for—only use I can see for 'em is to clean 'em off and save the canvas. And that's another thing—you'll not like the price. Once you go asking for something, that does it." He gave Richmond a sharp look. "Feared you mightn't pay up, thinking I'd cheated you, so I got receipts. Not much of a business man, as a rule, but can't afford to slip up now on a good commission." He laughed harshly. "Ironic, ain't it? The only worthwhile commission I can get in ten years is to purchase someone else's paintings—and a damned poor lot at that, or my name's not Jerry Bowles!"

"I'm sure you're right," acknowledged Richmond, walking over to the easel and inspecting the canvas which stood there." A portrait, eh? Your usual line?"

The painter shook his head. "No. I paint scenes, mostly, town scenes—life as I see it." He laughed harshly. "Not as most others do, seemingly—at least, not wealthy patrons."

Richmond nodded, studying the almost finished portrait without speaking. It showed a girl in ragged garments posed in a half-cringing, half-defiant attitude, one thin arm raised above her head as if to ward off a blow. Her pale, strained face was framed by dark, tangled hair which might have been pretty had it been washed and brushed. But it was the eyes which held Richmond's gaze; dark, tortured eyes which held a full knowledge of pain and a silent plea for a little kindness, a little love.

His face worked for a moment. The painter watched him curiously, then said quietly, "Not outside your experience, I notice."

"No." The monosyllable came with difficulty. There was a moment's pause before he continued in a more normal tone, "I'll buy this, when you've finished it."

The painter peered at him closely and whistled. "The devil you will! And what would a fine gentleman like yourself be wanting with the likes of her?"

Richmond's expression hardened. "She will remind me—should I need reminding."

Another man might have questioned what he meant; but the artist, like all his kind, could rely on his own perception to supply the answers.

"I notice you don't ask my price?"

"I'll pay it whatever it may be."

Bowles let out a lurid oath. "Now God damme for a prize fool, but I'll not ask for more than three guineas! The look on your face is payment enough—I see from it that I've succeeded in what I was trying for."

"It's the finest portrait I've ever seen. Make it three hundred guineas, and the bargain is struck."

"A madman, b'God! But if this is madness, then the devil fly away with sanity!" He looked shrewdly at Richmond once again. "And if I'm not mistaken, it isn't such a poor bargain from your point of view as one might suppose."

*　　　*　　　*

Not far away, in the gloomy chambers at Lincoln's Inn, Mr. Collins sat, checking the entries in a ledger. From time to time he looked up from his work, glancing sharply at the three clerks seated on the other side of the glass partition. Whenever one of them paused for a moment, or ventured to raise his head from its bowed position over the desk, he would tap smartly on the glass panel with a long ruler to indicate his disapprobation of this action.

"I loves ole Collins like a father, not arf I does," muttered the youngest of the clerks, out of the corner of his mouth.

The other two dared make no sign of having heard this sentiment, however much they may have agreed with it. All three continued to push their pens assiduously over the page. Mr. Collins watched for a few moments, his long nose twitching slightly; then, satisfied with their industry, he resumed his own work.

It was stuffy in the room, and the young clerk felt the sweat rising under his stiff collar. His thoughts went longingly to the pleasant green of the fields around Lincoln's Inn, of strolling there beneath the shady trees, watching the children at play and the pretty girls in soft, white dresses walking demurely with their elders. Spring, in fact, was working its old magic in his young blood.

It was a relief to him, therefore, to hear a knock on the outer door. He leapt up at once to answer it, and found a footman standing on the threshold.

"Mr. Collins?"

"No," replied the clerk, with a cheeky grin. "Name of Stubbs. But Mr. Collins is here, all right—worse luck," he added, in a much lower tone, "so you may leave that with me, if it's for him, as I suppose it is."

He gestured towards the letter in the man's hand.

"My instructions was," said the messenger, coldly, "to give this note into Mr. Collins's own hand, young man. So, if ye'll kindly direct me to the gentleman—"

"Have it your own way," replied the clerk, with a shrug, moving aside so that the visitor might enter.

In doing so, he almost stepped on the chief clerk's foot, for Collins had come up quietly behind him in order to discover why working time was being wasted. The lad was ordered sharply to his desk, while Collins took the note and dismissed the messenger with a nod, ignoring the latter's obvious disgust at being sent away without the expected payment for services rendered.

Retreating behind his partition, Collins opened the letter, studying it with an intensity of concentration which its brevity seemed scarcely to require. In fact, he read it through three times, changing colour slightly as he did so. Then he folded it again, placing it carefully in an inner pocket. He opened the lid of his desk to place inside the papers on which he had been working, shut the lid with a slam and locked it. This done, he rose, took his hat from a peg on the wall, and approached the desk where the three clerks were sitting.

"I have to go out," he said to the eldest of them, in a sharp tone. "See to it that you keep order here—and no slacking, mind. If Mr. Dally should ask for me, tell him that I shall be back in half an hour."

"Very good, Mr. Collins, sir."

With one searching look at the youngest clerk, Collins made for the door, donning his hat as he stepped outside.

He walked smartly out of Lincoln's Inn and along an alley that led to High Holborn, until he came to Will's Coffee House. Entering, he looked around.

As it was not a busy time of day there were plenty of vacant seats; he chose an isolated bench against the wall, and sat down to wait.

It was not for long—almost at once a man entered the shop and came towards him, taking a seat at his side on the bench.

"You're prompt off the mark, I see, Collins."

The clerk turned a pale face towards the newcomer, and his tone was ingratiating. "What do you want with me, Mr. Richmond, sir? I swear it's all a mistake, but I had to come to straighten things out—"

"Very wise," returned the other, dryly. "As for mistakes, we'll see about that. I wonder just how long you've been prying into your employer's locked deed boxes, passing on useful tit-bits concerning family wills and the like to interested parties? Quite some time, I'll wager, by the juicy little nest egg you've managed to accumulate." He paused to consider his companion for a moment with an expression of amused contempt. "Oh, yes, I have my methods," he continued. "But let's not waste time. You can now repeat to me the secret information which you passed on to Sir Sidney Chalfont not so very long ago."

"I don't know what you mean," stammered Collins.

Richmond sighed. "A pity. Had your understanding been more powerful, I intended to give you a chance to clear out, taking your ill-gotten gains with you, before I made Mr. Dally acquainted with your interesting activities. It goes against the grain to let a scoundrel like you get away with it, I must confess, but I don't doubt you'll get your deserts in the long run, anyway."

Collins put a hand up to loosen his collar, which had suddenly grown too tight. "You—you can't prove anything. The money—a man can save money—"

Richmond laughed shortly. "Out of your miserable wages? Oh, very likely! But there's more than that. You'll remember a man called Wynne? He's only awaiting my summons before he goes to lay certain facts about your dealings with him before Mr. Dally. You've bled him white, so he's nothing to lose now, and he's actuated by one of the most powerful motives in existence, Collins—revenge."

Collins said nothing for a few moments, his face working. "Supposing I tell you what you want to know," he said at last, in a choked voice. "Will you hold off this man Wynne?"

Richmond shook his head. "Can't be done. No, Collins, the best I can do is to give you the chance to run for it before the storm breaks. It's more than you deserve, but it's the price I'm prepared to pay for the information I want."

Scared as he was, Collins was still able to feel a twinge of curiosity. "What's it to you?" he demanded hoarsely. "I can't see any way it can assist you."

"Fortunately, that need not concern you, for there are a number of more urgent matters claiming your attention. You have two days in which to clear out—

that's if you tell me what I want to know. Otherwise—"
he pulled out his watch and consulted it—"shall we say
two hours—at the most?"

15

SIR SIDNEY PROPOSES

WHEN LADY VERWOOD heard of Diana's intention to
return home in a few days, she was dismayed.

"Oh, but surely not! You must wait until we have
given our ball—you know we agreed to have one, only
you have both been so occupied in attending other
people's, and then I was confident that we had plenty
of time! Pray, pray change your mind, dearest child!
At least wait another fortnight—we should be able to
arrange it all by then, I dare say, though it's not giving
people much notice, to be sure. Still that can't be
helped—"

Diana interrupted, gently but firmly insisting that she
must indeed go, as only yesterday she had learned from
Mr. Richmond, while they were all out riding, that he
intended to leave for Chesdene at the end of the week.

"How very tiresome!" exclaimed Lady Verwood. "Is
there nothing to be done?"

"Why yes, I have it!" Irene said, triumphantly. "You
shall give your ball, Aunt, for Diana's twenty-first
birthday next month, and she must come up to London
for it with her Mama! That will keep everybody
happy!"

Diana, reluctant to accept a favour of this kind from
someone who was not even distantly related to her,
began to make objections; but Lady Verwood was so

delighted with the scheme that it seemed positively ungracious to persist. Once the ball had been decided upon, both Irene and her aunt were more willing to allow Diana to leave when she saw fit. Her only anxiety now was how to avoid being obliged to travel home under her kinsman's escort.

It proved impossible, although she strained civility to its limits in repelling him. His natural claims as the head of the family were too strong, and she did not wish to antagonise him completely. She reminded herself that he could, if he chose, turn her mother and herself out of the Manor. So on Friday, having taken leave of her friends in London, she found herself seated opposite Sir Sidney Chalfont in his travelling coach, and heartily wishing either the gentleman or herself elsewhere.

At first, all went well. Sir Sidney seemed in a thoughtful mood and disinclined for conversation. After venturing a few polite commonplaces about the weather and the traffic, Diana thankfully took up the latest issue of *The Ladies' Magazine*, with which she had wisely provided herself before starting. Almost an hour went by in complete silence; now and again, Diana stole a surreptitious look at her escort, to find him either staring hard at the floor or out of the window. Once his eyes turned towards her. She quickly returned to her magazine and read with intense concentration that for full dress coloured crepe over white satin was at present very much esteemed in the world of fashion. There was much more on the same subject, and also a lively discussion on the various bonnets in vogue. Normally, she would have been genuinely interested in this information, but now it scarcely made any impression on her mind. She was becoming more and more uneasy at Sir Sidney's unusual silence and what it might portend.

She had just made up her mind to start a conversation herself rather than sit there any longer in that broody atmosphere, when he leaned forward and flicked her magazine with his finger.

"Pray put that away, Cousin Diana, for a moment, do. There's something I want to say most particularly to you."

She lowered the magazine and looked steadily at him, her eyes betraying nothing of her inward qualms.

"What may that be, Cousin?"

He fingered his cravat uneasily. "It's a devilish difficult thing to start on," he mumbled. "Fact is, I wish I knew where I stood with you. It might be easier then."

She thought she knew what was coming and her heart gave an unpleasant thud.

"Where you stand with me?" she repeated, trying to sound puzzled.

"Yes. It's that fellow Langley, y'see. Thing is, I can see he's head over heels in love with you—any fool could, for that matter—but the question is, what d'you think of him?"

"Oh!"

She gave a sigh of relief. For a moment, she had feared . . . But no, evidently Irene had been right, after all. She had insisted that Sir Sidney's recent access of interest in his kinswoman was no doubt due to his having come belatedly to a sense of his obligations towards her in his role as head of the family. An important part of those obligations would be to inquire into the intentions of any aspirants to her hand. She sighed again, this time with exasperation. She did not in the least want him to take an interest in her concerns. She had managed very well on her own all these years, and it would be a constant source of irritation if she had to be answerable to someone else from now onwards. She must be tactful, of course, but she decided to give him a hint of her feelings on this score.

"Oh, pray don't concern yourself over that, sir!" she finished with a shrug. "As a matter of fact, you need not bother to concern yourself with my affairs at all—though it is very good of you to do so, of course," she added, hastily.

"Think nothing of it, cos.," he assured her, with a rather sickly smile. "Fact is, I think a deuce of a lot of

you, you know, and I want to concern myself with
your affairs—ask nothing better, in fact—"

She did not like the sound of this, and hastened to
cut in. "Yes, but, you see, I have been so used to fend
for myself in the past that I don't really take too
kindly, I fear, to anyone else interf—, that is to say,
trying to assist me or advise me in any way. While my
father was still alive, he left Mama and me pretty much
to our own devices; and since then, we have been completely on our own, for we did not choose to accept the
help of my uncle, Mama's brother. And I am not a raw
girl—I shall be one and twenty next month, as you are
aware. So you see, Cousin, although it is most kind on
your part, there is really no need for you to feel that
you must watch over and protect me, for I am very
well able to look after myself."

"Ay, so you may think, Cousin, but it don't do for
females to be looking after themselves—not at all the
thing. But that's not altogether what I meant. What I
mean is—oh, devil take it! Do you, or do you not,
have any thought of marrying young Langley?"

Diana's chin went up a little. "I suppose I can
scarcely object to the question, in view of your position
as head of the family," she replied, coldly.

"Oh, as to that, I may as well tell you I've a closer
interest in your answer than that of a mere guardian.
But don't keep me in suspense any longer—d'you care
for the fellow?"

"Well, since you will have it—no, not in any way
that would make me consider marriage. And I am not
at all sure that Mark thinks of me in that way, either.
It is true that he has a certain amount of—of admiration for me, but I have always thought of it as nothing
more than a boy's callow feelings for the first female
whom he comes to know really well—I have never
thought it the basis for a lasting attachment."

Sir Sidney nodded wisely. "Calf love," he pronounced. "Most of us suffer from it, one time or another."

"Exactly so. And already I think I see signs of a

more stable attachment springing up in another quarter."

"You mean the little filly who's been with you a great deal since you came to town—what's her name? Rathbone, that's it."

"Yes."

"Not a bad match for either side," said Sir Sidney, reflectively. "Langley's father's a warm man, shouldn't wonder. Missed your chance there, Cousin, if you don't mind my saying so—deuced glad you did, though."

"If you suppose," began Diana, indignantly, "that I am the kind of female who would take advantage of a boy's temporary infatuation to further my own ends—"

"Don't see why not," interrupted Sir Sidney, in a reasoning tone. "People do it all the time—only thing for a female *to* do, come to think of it, when she's no one else to provide for her. Only thing for a man to do, what's more, when he's hard pressed. Way of the world, cousin Diana. Deuce take it!" he exclaimed suddenly. "Can't we drop this calling each other 'cousin', and get down to simple Christian names? I ain't your cousin, only by a remove, anyway. What d'you say? Any objection if I call you Diana?"

She hesitated, but could think of no valid reason for refusing this request. "Very well, if you wish," she said at last, reluctantly.

"Capital! It will make everything much easier. And I can't tell you how relieved I am to learn that you've no intention of making a match of it with young Langley. Fact is, Diana, my dear—oh, deuce take it!" he exclaimed, impatiently, as she made a move to raise her magazine again, "can't you put that confounded thing down, and give me your full attention for a moment?"

She threw the magazine aside, resigning herself to the inevitable. Perhaps it was better to get it over once and for all.

"You must have seen how it is with me— I'm fairly bowled over, and no two ways about it. And what could be more suitable than a match between us? You've been mistress of Chesdene Manor for long enough—"

Diana shook her head. "No, my Mama is—or was—"

He shrugged this aside. "Comes to the same thing. Yours is the guiding hand, Diana, it don't take a genius to see that. Not that I'd wish to live in the place, mind you, after we're wed—London's my natural habitat. But the old—that's to say, your mother—could continue there with my right good will, and maybe we could find a tenant for the rest of it, if we did it up a trifle. I must say, that was a good notion of yours, though I'm not so struck on this fellow Richmond. Still, he'll be gone soon enough; and as I collect he's made a few improvements in the house, no harm done. Come to think of it, with a small outlay on further necessary improvements—nothing too drastic, mind, for the damned place could swallow up a fortune in no time—we might get quite a tidy income from letting it," he went on, reflectively. "It's a handsome house—from the outside, at all events, and would make a respectable gentleman's residence—for a respectable gentleman, that is, and that's something I don't set up to be, eh, me dear?" He laughed heartily. "Well, what d'you say?"

"About your being a respectable gentleman, sir?"

He let out a shout of laughter. "No, damme! You're trying to gammon me, you saucy miss!" He leaned towards her, and tried to take her hand, but she snatched it away. "Devil take it, Diana, don't be missish—I've made a declaration, all right and tight—now, what d'ye say?"

She felt considerably embarrassed, but forced herself to answer in a calm, matter-of-fact tone.

"Naturally, I am very sensible of the honour. But you must see, Sir Sidney, that it would not do at all. I—you—" she faltered a little, then went on, recovering her poise—"we are such very different kinds of people."

"How d'ye reckon that? It's my belief we've a deal in common—Chesdene, the name—even, yes even our temperaments, damme! You're a bit of a high-stepper,

for a female, Diana, don't try to tell me you're not!
And so am I—oh, yes, we'd suit all right, never a
doubt of it."

"Do you think so? Well, I do not," she answered,
flatly. "And if I may say so, Cousin, talking of high-
stepping, I had no notion that you could afford a
wife—at least, not one such as I, without a dowry."

"Not one such as—" He broke off, took a deep
breath and laughed again. "Well, you speak plain,
ma'am, I'll give you that. But love, you know, disre-
gards such paltry matters as dowries. You are—yes,
damme, you're a fortune in yourself! And any man
would be glad to take you without a penny to your
name!"

She inclined her head in a graceful little bow.

"I thank you for the compliment. But even setting
aside such mundane matters as how we should contrive
to live—"

He made an impatient gesture. "Haven't I told you
we could make a very tidy sum from the Manor? But
it's not for females to bother their pretty heads with
such stuff—only say yes, and you can safely leave everything else to me."

"Well, that's just it, Sir Sidney. I regret that I
haven't the smallest inclination to say yes."

A look of deep chagrin came over his face, to be replaced by a scowl and an angry flush.

"What's this? You refuse me? Why? You say you
don't care a pin for young Langley—"

"I don't care for any man," she interrupted him,
quietly. "And that's why I must decline your offer."

For a moment, he looked as though he might burst
into a violent display of temper. He managed to control
himself, however.

"I see how it is," he said, at last, with a shrug. "You
need more time—I've been too sudden. No elegant
female can bring herself to accept on the first applica-
tion, after all. I'll try to be patient, but don't keep me
waiting too long, there's a good girl, for I detest delay
in anything that matters to me."

"Upon my word," exclaimed Diana, feeling her own temper rising, "I don't know what I should say that will make my feelings more clear to you! Let me inform you that I certainly don't aspire to the kind of elegance that trifles with a man on such a subject! I do not wish to marry you, and I can't suppose that any amount of time would make any difference to my inclinations in that direction. There! Have I said enough to convince you, now?"

He glared at her for a moment. She met his gaze evenly enough, though inwardly she experienced some qualms. After a while, his eyes dropped away from hers, and she picked up her magazine again with hands that trembled very slightly.

"Well, you've not been very civil," he said, in a surly tone. "But we'll say no more about it at present, if that's your wish. I can wait."

She bit back the angry retort that rose to her lips, and pretended to be absorbed in her magazine. He let her alone, and nothing more was said between them until they alighted at the door of Chesdene Manor.

16

TEA WITH MR. RICHMOND

FOR SOME reason not quite clear to herself, Diana said nothing to her mother of Sir Sidney's proposal of marriage. Privately, she puzzled over it a good deal. Try as she would, she could not bring herself to believe that her kinsman was genuinely in love with her; but if not, then what on earth could be his reason for wishing to marry her? He had nothing at all to gain from the match. Chesdene Manor was already his, and she had neither property nor fortune of her own. Everything she had heard in London confirmed her previous supposition that he was rapidly gaming away his substance even as her own father had done in his lifetime. If he married for anything but love, it must surely be for money. The more she thought about it, the more extraordinary it appeared.

The one beneficial result of the scene between them was that Sir Sidney left her alone for a few days. His original intention had been to stay overnight at the Manor with his relatives, but he abandoned this, going straight to the King's Arms in the nearby town. He informed Diana that he expected to be joined there in a day or two by his friend Harnby.

"And don't think you've seen the last of me, my dear girl," he whispered in her ear, as he took leave of her after delivering her safely to her mother. "I don't take my dismissal seriously, damme if I do. In spite of all you may say now, I'll wager you'll come round in time."

She made no answer to this, judging it a waste of time; but the prospect of further applications, supported no doubt by the odious Mr. Harnby, somewhat daunted even her intrepid spirit. She had already strained civility to the utmost in making her feelings plain to him. To go further might result in his turning her mother and herself out of the Manor. It was an intolerable position.

Fortunately, her mind was very soon distracted from the problem by the news that Mr. Richmond had returned.

"When did he come?" she asked her mother.

"Only yesterday. The place has been in quite a bustle ever since the workmen finished, what with furniture arriving, and packages of all shapes and sizes—not to speak of a manservant and his wife who have been interviewing girls from the village as housemaids and so forth. Our tenant has set up quite an establishment here, by what I can see of things."

"Has he invited you in to inspect the improvements, Mama?"

"He paid a civil call upon me yesterday shortly after he arrived, and suggests that, when you returned, we might both like to look in and take tea with him one afternoon."

"I shall certainly accept the invitation, for I don't mind telling you that I am bursting with curiosity!"

"Why, so am I, my love, but I trust I managed to conceal it. However, he must think a little curiosity justified, for in a way we are responsible to Sir Sidney for any alterations that are made in what is, after all, his house."

Mention of Sir Sidney had the effect of making Diana change the subject quickly; and as she had much to tell her mother about the London visit, this presented no difficulty.

They saw nothing of their neighbour either that day or on the succeeding one, when they walked over to Latimer House to visit Mr. and Mrs. Langley. The Langleys were delighted to see them and to have news of Irene and Mark to supplement the letters which arrived with reasonable frequency from London. Mrs. Langley showed an inclination to question Diana closely about the Rathbones.

"Are they a pleasant family? I collect from Irene's letters that the mother is a bit of a dragon, athough my sister is very friendly with her. But then, no one could accuse poor Maria of being critical of others—she is the most good-natured person in the world."

Diana agreed whole-heartedly with this, adding that the Rathbones had been most amiable towards Lady Verwood's visitors, but that perhaps Mrs. Rathbone was at times a little unfeeling towards her youngest child.

"Ah, yes, a daughter, Letitia, is it not? Both Irene and Mark have mentioned her a great deal in their letters. What do you think of her, my dear?"

"She's a charming girl," replied Diana, without hesitation. "Completely unaffected, but a little shy and uncertain of herself. It's scarcely surprising considering the way she is constantly compared unfavourably with her sisters."

"Yes, Mark mentioned that circumstance. I had the impression—" she paused a moment, looking uncertainly at Diana, as though she feared to hurt her feelings—"I may be wrong, but I felt from what he said that he was developing a rather particular interest in the young lady."

"I must say, ma'am, that the same thought had crossed my mind, seeing them together. But there's no saying how such things may go. A young man of Mark's age is very impressionable."

"Upon my word," laughed Mrs. Langley, "you make it sound as if you were the elder, instead of its being the other way about!"

"Do I? But I have always felt myself to be years older than your son, you see. In fact," concluded Diana, with a wry smile, "I sometimes seem a very Methuselah compared to others of my age, or thereabouts. Perhaps I am old maidish."

Both Mrs. Langley and Diana's mother protested at this.

"How can you say so?" asked Lady Chalfont, indignantly. "Why, you are by far too lively for that!"

"And too handsome, my dear child," put in Mr. Langley, who had entered the room a moment since in time to hear the last few remarks. "If you aspire to being an old maid, I fear I must warn you that you've very little hope of it."

She smiled, but shook her head. Plenty of young men had shown an interest in her in London, but she had never for a moment been tempted to think their attentions serious. Who would want to wed a penniless female, after all? In spite of herself, she sighed. It was ironical that the only man who had proposed marriage to her was one in whom she felt not the slightest interest.

On the following morning a message came from Mr. Richmond inviting the ladies to do him the honour of paying a call that afternoon to inspect his apartments. They sent back an acceptance; and at the appointed time, full of curiosity, presented themselves at his door.

He opened it himself. After a few moments spent in civil greetings, they were able to look about them and see what changes he had made in the entrance hall. It had lost its musty, disused smell, and a cheerful fire burned in the huge grate, dispelling the coldness of the stone-flagged floor. The walls, previously streaked with the dirt of years, were now freshly painted in a delicate shade of green; and the beautiful plasterwork of the ceiling once more showed to advantage.

"Why!" exclaimed Lady Chalfont involuntarily. "I don't recall seeing it look like this since you were quite a little girl, Diana! And oddly enough, it was the same colour, then. How much better it looks, too, with some pictures hung!"

She walked over to the wall, to inspect the pictures more closely. Diana followed, and after glancing at one or two, turned away with a slight feeling of disappointment. She could not quite tell why, but she had somehow expected that their tenant would have had better taste in art. Most of the pictures were portraits, a few were landscapes; all were equally without distinction.

She glanced at her mother, to see how she was taking it, and was surprised by the expression on Lady Chalfont's face. For her mother was moving from one picture to another with what was obviously an ever-growing bewilderment. At length she spoke.

"But, Mr. Richmond—I don't know, surely I can't be mistaken, but after all these years—but that man in the periwig, for instance—yes, of course I remember him, he was Sir Charles Chalfont, one of my husband's ancestors! And this landscape—such a dreary thing as I used to think it, though naturally I never dared say so in Sir John's hearing—" she broke off, and took a deep breath. "Mr. Richmond, I don't know how it can be so, for I know they were all sold long ago—but surely most of these, if not all, are the selfsame pictures that used to hang here when Sir John was alive?"

He nodded his dark head briefly. "That is so, ma'am."

"But how did you know?" she gasped, while Diana, too, stared at him. "And how did you manage to find them again, after all this time?"

"There are such things as inventories of sales, Lady Chalfont."

"Oh—oh, yes. I suppose so, though I know nothing of the matter, really. But—but—it is all so extraordinary—"

"I must confess," said Diana, in her usual candid manner, "that I should have expected you to prefer pictures of your own choice."

"Hush, child!" reproved her mother, hastily. "Mr. Richmond is under no obligation to explain his decisions to us."

"Nevertheless, ma'am, I am ready to do so. My object was to restore these apartments as nearly as possible to their original state."

"Why?" demanded Diana, bluntly.

"Why?" he considered for a moment. "Say that it pleased my fancy."

"But how could you know," she persisted, "what they were like originally? I don't remember so much myself except for an odd thing here and there."

He shrugged. "If one is determined to discover anything, there are always sources of information."

"What sources?"

"Ah, Miss Chalfont, you can't expect an artist in any form to reveal the inspiration of his art."

"Well, I suppose you would call restoration an art," she said, doubtfully, smiling in response to his quizzical tone.

"Certainly."

"But someone must have told you—who, I wonder? Who was familiar with the house when Grandfather was alive, apart from Mama? Was it—I know!" she exclaimed, triumphantly. "It was Mr. Dally! I never thought of him!"

"I knew your quick wits would find a solution at last," he replied, smiling.

"Well, am I right—was it Mr. Dally?"

He shook his head again. "I prefer to keep it a mystery, ma'am, then I'm in no danger of losing your interest in viewing my work. Would you care to pass on—to the library, for instance?"

"Well, one thing you can't have done," she said, with satisfaction, "is to have replaced the original volumes on the shelves. We have the best of them in our wing of the house."

He gave her an amused look. "Not the originals, perhaps. But one can always buy copies of the same books, you know."

He opened the door of the library, and stood aside to allow them to enter.

Diana looked critically about her. In contrast to the hall, this room was warmed by the sun, which streamed through the mullioned windows, imparting a mellow glow to the dark oak panelling which lined the lower part of the walls. A thick red carpet covered the floor, so that footsteps were muffled: gold brocade curtains framed the windows, and the cushions of the window seat had been tastefully covered in gold and red striped satin. The old wing chairs had been removed, and two sturdier specimens put in their place.

She glanced at these and smiled reminiscently. Looking up, she noticed Richmond's eyes upon her and saw that he was smiling, too. It flashed across her mind that he rarely smiled as now, with genuine amusement, and that when he did, it transformed his face. Most of his smiles were wry, ironical twists of the mouth which only served to accentuate a certain sombre expression that seemed habitual to him. She reflected that possibly this was because of his dark complexion and hair. His eyes, too, were very nearly black, and had a piercing intensity which could almost make one feel uncomfortable at times.

"It's charming," she said, sincerely. Then, altering

her tone—"And at least you need not fear to sit in these chairs, I imagine!"

"They're as safe as the Bank of England," he promised her, still smiling. "Would you care to try them? I assure you that I don't suggest it in order to get my own back on you."

"What nonsense is this?" demanded Lady Chalfont, with a laugh and a puzzled look first at one, then the other. "It seems you have some secret joke between you."

"Don't you remember, Mama? I did tell you about it, when the Langleys were with us, after Mr. Richmond had called to see the house for the first time. Mark was highly amused—"

"Oh, yes," interposed her mother, quickly, with an anxious look at their host. "I do remember now. You had an unfortunate mishap with one of those old chairs, did you not? Most distressing for you, Mr. Richmond, and I would not like you to think that we were all so heartless as to laugh at your discomfiture—"

"You may do so, ma'am, with my right good will," said Richmond, "any time that I choose to make a fool of myself, as I did then."

"What, any time?" queried Diana, with a saucy look.

"Now, now, Diana! Pray mind your tongue! You must not heed her, Mr. Richmond; she means no offence, really, but she has this lively way of speech, and I'm always warning her that it may give strangers a very odd opinion of her. Her old friends are used to it, you know, and pay no heed. But to others, it must seem—"

Diana grimaced. "Oh, Mama! Must you apologise for my conduct? I am almost one and twenty, and can be supposed to be answerable for myself."

"Not to me, Miss Chalfont. Your style exactly suits my own." The dark eyes met hers levelly for a moment, and she felt a quick stirring of excitement within her. "But what do you think of my books, I wonder?"

She turned to the shelves, glad to be released from

the unexpected magnetism of his eyes. She found his taste in books more commendable than she had thought his taste in art, but for once refrained from speaking her mind on this point. It was true that she saw there many titles which could be found in her own small collection in the Dowager's Wing, but there were others, too, among them several which she would have liked to own. Evidently, in this instance the tenant had not concentrated exclusively on restoring things as they had been in the past. Perhaps, she thought, he had lacked precise enough information to do so.

According to Lady Chalfont, however, the dining-room was exactly as she remembered it. The handsome green damask paper and intricate plasterwork of the ceiling gave the room an elegance which Diana could never have credited. Richmond gestured towards the dark oak refectory table, and grimaced.

"I must confess I feel a shade formal, sitting alone at what seems to be at least a mile of table. When I'm not entertaining, I shall most likely take my meals on a small table in the parlour—that's if my manservant will permit it. He's a deuced starchy fellow."

"Oh, you mean the small parlour overlooking the garden, I take it?" asked Lady Chalfont. "Of course, you would scarcely bother to do up the large drawing-room on the first floor. It was once a very handsome apartment." She sighed nostalgically. "I can't think why it was that my husband never cared for this house," she went on. "At least, I suppose it was simply because he disliked living in the country. But when Sir John was still alive and it was properly cared for, it really was a beautiful home. I remember her father saying, Diana, that your Uncle Ralph ought to have been the one to inherit, for he always loved the place. I don't know about that myself, for poor Ralph had been dead seven years when I married your father, and I never met him. But his wife used to say it, too—poor little Amelia."

"Certainly one does realise what a handsome house it once was, seeing the difference made in it by Mr.

Richmond's improvements," admitted Diana. "I cannot remember a time when it wasn't shabby and neglected—but then I was only eight when Grandfather died, and we came here so seldom in those days. After that, I never set eyes on it again until Papa brought us up here to live."

"And do you like living here?" asked Richmond. "Or would you prefer to be in London, where I collect you've spent most of your life?"

"Oh, here!" answered Diana, without the smallest hesitation. "I like living in the country, and besides—" She hesitated for a moment, then continued, "I don't know if it's because I'm a Chalfont, and the Manor has been the home of Chalfonts for centuries, but I have a certain proprietorial feeling . . . Stupid, of course," she finished, with a shrug which did not entirely conceal her emotion. "It isn't mine—never can be."

Richmond glanced at Lady Chalfont, who had moved a little apart from them to inspect a classical figure standing in one of the niches.

"Unless you were to marry the owner," he said, quietly.

Diana felt her colour rising. "That is not at all likely," she replied coldly.

"I must confess I had thought—but naturally it is no concern of mine. Pray forgive me."

He spoke more loudly, to include Lady Chalfont. "And now if you will step into the parlour, ladies, I'll see if my housekeeper can supply us with some tea."

The parlour was a small oak panelled room, bright with sunlight and tastefully furnished. Almost at once, Diana's eye was caught by a large picture, the only one to be displayed on the wall opposite the fireplace. It was the portrait for which Richmond had paid three hundred guineas.

She considered it in silence for some time. Her mother was fluently expressing delight at the furnishings of the room while Richmond listened politely, although his eyes were on Diana. At last, he showed Lady Chalfont to a chair, and turned to her daughter.

"What do you think of that?" he asked, nodding towards the picture.

"I—I'm not sure. It's a very—unusual picture. I can't say I like it exactly, but it has the power to make one feel intense pity for the subject. Why did you purchase it, sir? Was it one of the originals?"

"Not to my knowledge," put in Lady Chalfont, turning her eyes towards the subject of the discussion. "I am positive I never set eyes on it before, for it is not a picture one could forget. I hope you will not mind, Mr. Richmond, if I say that I do not care for it overmuch. It makes one feel quite uncomfortable, I declare!"

"That is what the artist had in mind, ma'am. I bought it because it had something to say, and I take that to be the purpose of art. Also—"

He paused. They looked at him expectantly.

"It put me in mind," he finished, slowly, "of something I was perhaps in danger of forgetting."

There was a moment's uncomfortable silence. He moved to the fireplace and pulled the bell rope.

"Pray be seated, Miss Chalfont," he invited Diana, with a smile. "These chairs, too, are quite reliable, I assure you."

Her answering smile was absent-minded. She was puzzling over his previous remark.

17

A Sprat to Catch a Mackerel

IT COULD not be claimed that Sir Sidney Chalfont was a particularly perceptive man, but even he felt a little dashed by Diana's reception of his proposal of marriage. He admitted as much to Harnby on the following day, when his friend and creditor arrived at the King's Arms to join him.

"Can't think what ails the wench," he finished in an aggrieved tone, after he had given an account of his conversation with Diana on the journey from Town. "She admits that fellow Langley means nothing to her and says there's no one else. What's more, she can't expect to engage anyone else's serious attentions in her situation—she knows the time o' day, all right, does my cousin Diana. So what's she at? You don't suppose," he went on, in a slightly alarmed tone, "that she's any inkling of what's in the wind?"

The other man looked at him contemptuously.

"No—how should she? It's been a close kept secret for long enough. The thing is, you're not much of a hand at courtship."

"Well, I like that!" replied Chalfont explosively. "After I've worn myself to a shadow playing the gallant, paying idiotic compliments, looking at her like a mooncalf, neglecting the tables so that I could trip around the floor with her at one of the damned flattest assemblies I was ever at in my life—"

"I'm not saying you didn't do your best," acknowledged Harnby, magnanimously. "Thing is, your best wasn't good enough. Ain't you had any experience with females?"

"Experience!" snorted Chalfont. "Don't be damned insulting—of course I've had experience! But not with females of my cousin Diana's quality. I've never been in the marrying line, you should know that. Bits of muslin are another matter."

"Well, it's no use holding an inquest. Never does any good over a game of cards, and love affairs are much the same come to think of it. Thing is, you've failed, and now we must think of something else."

"I haven't failed—at least, not yet. Oh, I know she refused me, but lots of girls do that the first time they're asked. Know heaps of instances, in my own family, too. My Aunt Lavinia, so I've heard my mother say—"

"For God's sake, Chalfont, I didn't travel hot-foot from London to hear about your Aunt Lavinia, or any of the rest of your repulsive family! I came—"

"Well, that's the outside of enough!" exclaimed his companion, angrily. "First you insult me, then it's my family. I tell you what, Harnby, for two pins, I'd break with you altogether. Don't like your style, lately, I don't mind telling you."

"Like it or lump it, it'll take more than two pins to buy my quittance, and don't you forget it," Harnby reminded him, ominously. "If it's slipped your mind, I have a record of the exact sum—"

"Oh, all right, all right! No need to turn up rough, only you can't expect a man to take insults lying down. And, anyway, I don't think it's quite hopeless with my cousin. She says there's no one else, and that's encouraging, at any rate, you must admit."

"I don't know," said Harnby, thoughtfully. "She might say that, but is it true? Seemed to me, the little I saw of them together, there was something between her and that Nabob fellow—what's 'is name?"

"You mean Chertsey's friend Richmond?" asked Chalfont incredulously. "Good God man, the notion's absurd! Why, they've only met in a business way, so to speak, and I don't think she likes him above half. Fellow's too damned mysterious. He's a friend of Chertsey's and everyone knows Chertsey, of course, so he's accepted, but after all, what's anyone know about him?"

Harnby stared at him thoughtfully for a moment. "Yes," he said, at last, reflectively. "What does anyone know about him? I've a notion, my dear Chalfont, that it might not be such a very bad thing to rectify that lack of information."

"Well, yes, I've thought as much myself, and said so to Diana, though she feels that as the lawyer is satisfied—"

"Collins," murmured Harnby, in a considering tone.

"No, perhaps not. It's easy enough to supply false credentials, after all. No, I think perhaps the answer is to look for our information among his private effects."

Sir Sidney goggled. "His private effects? Have you taken leave of your senses, Ferdy? How d'ye suggest we do it?"

"Quite simple," replied Harnby, airily. "Well, comparatively, at least. We must search his rooms at the Manor."

"Search—!" Chalfont stared aghast. "Well, now I know there *are* bats in your belfry! Comparatively simple, you say? Compared with what? Lifting the Crown Jewels?"

"Ingenuity is all that's required, my dear chap. There's aways a way if one uses one's wits."

"Not for me," declared Sir Sidney, with unexpected firmness. "I don't object to a bit of sleight of hand, provided one can come through without losing credit; but I've no notion of embarking on a nick-purse scheme such as this. Damme, I'm a Chalfont, after all!"

"And your ancestors, of course, were all models of integrity," sneered Harnby.

"Well not that precisely, but—oh, for God's sake, Ferdy! We should never bring it off, and what purpose would it serve, anyway? It won't further my suit with Diana."

"Unless I am right and you're wrong, and she does have a fancy for him. In that case, it would help you a good deal if you could set her against him."

"But how do we know we'd find anything of that kind?" insisted Sir Sidney. "Fellow may have led a blameless life, for all we can tell."

"Young men aren't usually packed off to the Indies unless their families want to get rid of them for some good reason. No, it seems to me a hopeful avenue of inquiry. Moreover, if it did turn out as we hope, it would reinforce my other plan."

"Other plan?" asked Sir Sidney, a trifle nervously.

Harnby nodded. "Yes—I've been turning one over

in my mind, and it seems to me I've hit on the very thing to advance you in the lady's favour. How do you fancy yourself as a kind of St. George?"

Chalfont laughed. "I don't see myself as any kind of saint—nor do you, unless you really are wanting in the top storey, which I begin to suspect! Out with it, man, what is this plan?"

Harnby leaned forward in his chair. "Why, simply that you shall rescue your kinswoman from some danger, thereby earning her heartfelt gratitude. Gratitude is a good start towards a more tender emotion."

"Danger? What danger?"

"Well that's something we'll have to work out. Oh, never fear—" as he saw the alarm growing in his companion's expression—"it will be staged, you know. Only your cousin will think it real. She could perhaps be held up by highwaymen—"

Chalfont gave a shout of laughter.

"Highwaymen! That's rich, Ferdy! What sort of gulls d'you imagine would trouble to hold up a gig— and that's the only kind of carriage Diana keeps at Chesdene. Rich pickings they'd expect from the owner of such a handsome turn-out, to be sure! Good God, what a brilliant notion! My cousin Diana would smell a rat at once—I tell you, she's really up to snuff, that girl."

"Very well," replied Harnby, in an offended tone. "You think of something then. How could I be expected to know that the ladies of Chesdene Manor travel about the neighbourhood in such shabby style?"

"No, of course not," agreed Chalfont, pleased with himself for gaining the initiative for a moment, and ready to be magnanimous in consequence. "And it's not such a bad notion—apart from the accident of its being a gig, of course. I collect you mean these gentlemen of the High Toby to be hirelings of ours? D'ye happen to know any highwaymen, Ferdy? Can't say I do, and I know some devilish rum customers."

"I don't, as a matter of fact, but that's irrelevant, in

the circumstances. Very well, then, she can be set on by footpads—or poachers, even—"

Sir Sidney sat up suddenly. "Ah, now, that's more like it!" he exclaimed. "I understand she often goes walking in the woods that lead down from the back of the Manor—when she goes over to see the Langleys, for instance. And I collect that more often than not, she's alone on these jaunts. Now, if we could discover a suitable moment—"

"And have a couple of men lurking nearby, ready to attack—"

"Mind you," said Chalfont, turning on him, "there mustn't be any real harm done— I can't agree to anything like that. These men must be given very strict instructions not to hurt anyone."

"Don't worry, they will be. They won't disarrange a hair of her head—"

"Not only hers," put in Chalfont hurriedly. "Mine too. I'm no hand at a bout of fisticuffs, I don't mind telling you."

"That's all very well," objected Harnby, "but you'll have to give the semblance of a fight, at any rate, or otherwise she'll definitely suspect something—if she's as spry as you think she is."

"Devil take it! I suppose you're right. Very well, then, I might perhaps beat them off with my cane—but see to it that they understand not to put up too much resistance."

Harnby reassured him on this point, and in a little while Chalfont came round to thinking that the plan was not such a bad one, after all.

"When shall we try it?" he asked.

"That will depend on when a suitable moment presents itself. But we must be ready—and, remember, there's no time to waste. We have barely a month."

"What about these ruffians? Shall we employ local talent?"

Harnby shook his head. "Much better to hire them in London. Plenty of 'em about in the East End. Leave that side of the business to me. Yours is to keep a watch on the girl, and pass the word on when she's likely to go for a stroll in the woods alone."

"It'll cost a bit," demurred Chalfont, doubtfully. "Fetching these men from Town, lodgin' 'em, paying their hire—"

"Can't make an omelette without breaking eggs, my dear chap. Or should I say—" he smiled in an unpleasant way—"it needs a sprat to catch a mackerel?"

18

THE EMPTY BOX

RICHMOND RODE at a gentle trot down the hill that led from Latimer and reined in his horse on the humpbacked bridge over the Chess. It was a fine morning, with a sportive breeze which wafted white wisps of clouds across the blue sky and stirred the trees, fresh in their spring green. He halted there for a few moments, watching the sun glinting on the water and the antics of the ducks from nearby Mill Farm. After a while, he lifted his eyes to the patchwork green slopes of the Chilterns, and a surge of fierce pride filled his heart. This was his country, and every fibre of his being responded to it. No dramatic scenery, with towering mountains, deep ravines and tempestuous torrents, but a gentle, rolling landscape of neat hedgerows and fields bright with wild flowers, or green with springing corn; a calm, domestic landscape where hamlets nestled in the valleys and sheep grazed on the hillsides.

After a while, his horse began to fidget, and he rode on. He usually went round by way of the road which skirted the wood and led to the village green; today, acting on impulse, he took the pathway through the wood. This came out into a narrow lane which ran beside the wall surrounding Chesdene Manor.

He was nearing the end of the ride when he saw the flutter of a muslin skirt ahead of him. At the same moment its wearer must have heard his approach, for she looked round, hesitating a moment. He quickened the horse's pace until he drew level to discover that the lady was Miss Chalfont. She was wearing a simple blue and white muslin gown, and had evidently grown tired of her bonnet, for it dangled by its ribbons from one negligent hand. As he reined in beside her she looked up, the dappled sunlight catching the reddish tints in her brown hair. His heart lifted again as it had done a few moments since, when he stood on the bridge; this time, it was a woman's beauty that moved him.

He gave no sign of his feelings, but nodded and calmly wished her good morning, remarking on the fine weather.

"Yes, isn't it a lovely day?" she agreed. "I've been calling on the Langleys. I received a letter from Irene this morning, and I knew Mrs. Langley would want to hear it without delay. We always share our letters," she added, with a laugh, "whenever Irene goes away on a visit. Today it was my turn."

He had been prepared to ride on, not wishing to intrude where possibly he was not wanted; but her friendly manner encouraged him to dismount.

"May I escort you the rest of the way?" he asked.

"Why, of course—but it's only a step. Still, we are going to the same place, after all," she replied, smiling.

"Do you often walk in the woods alone?" he asked, as he led his horse beside her.

"Oh, yes, why not? Almost every day, when the weather's fine. I suppose," she added, a trifle scornfully, "you are thinking it isn't proper for me to go unattended. But we don't regard such things in the country—it is altogether different in Town, of course."

"I wasn't thinking of propriety, as a matter of fact."

"Then what were you thinking of, sir? Safety, perhaps?" She laughed. "I assure you, I am as safe here as in the parlour at home. Who should harm me in Chesdene?"

He made no reply for a moment, and she looked at him in surprise.

"You are probably right," he said, eventually. "How are your friends faring in London? I trust you have good news of them?"

"The best!" she exclaimed, eagerly. "I'm sure I may tell you, for I know you are discreet; besides, as Mr. Chertsey is a close friend of yours, he will certainly tell you himself before long. What do you think? He and Irene are engaged to be married! That is, they will be, when he has gained her parents' consent. He is coming here in a day or two to get their answer—when I took them the letter from Irene this morning, I found they had also received one from her and from Mr. Chertsey, by the same post. You can imagine how we talked and talked about the whole affair! And Mama will be so sorry to have missed it all because she had an appointment with the dressmaker, and wasn't able to accompany me. Still, it's no matter, because they are calling on us this afternoon—although some of the excitement will have worn off by then. It's always the first burst of good news that's so pleasurable, don't you think?"

He agreed with her gravely, and added, "I can't say I am prodigiously surprised at the news, though."

"No, it was fairly obvious before we left London, wasn't it? Oh, I am so glad for Irene! And I think they will be admirably suited—he seems so full of enthusiasm and spirits, while Irene is a little on the quiet side. I think it should be like that, don't you, so that one is a complement of the other? Or do you feel that partners should be of a similar temperament?"

He had been studying her face as she talked, following the changing expressions which flitted across it like the shafts of sunlight he had watched rippling on the surface of the river. He thought again how lovely she was, how bright and vital ... Suddenly there rose before his mind's eye the image of the picture hanging in his parlour at the Manor. That girl, and this one—what right had she to be so free and happy, while the other had known the hell of slavery and misery? He must not forget . . .

He pulled himself back from a vast distance.

"I fear I've never given the matter a moment's thought," he said, brusquely.

She was somewhat taken aback by his tone, but her mood was too genial to be much affected by it. "Oh, have you not? How strange! Most people think of marriage at some time in their lives."

"And have you?"

A faint flush touched her cheek. "Oh, yes, in a general way," she replied, hesitantly.

"But never in a particular one?"

"Mr. Richmond," she said, with deliberately forced archness, "you know very well you have no right to put such a question to any lady! It is vastly impertinent of you, sir!"

"You are right, of course. I beg your pardon. But pray don't play-act with me, Miss Chalfont. I can take a straight reproof, and one of the qualities I most respect in you is your sincerity. Most females are such artificial creatures."

"Thank you," she replied, in a mocking tone. "But I don't care to accept a compliment made at the expense of the remainder of my sex. I suspect you're a woman-hater, sir!"

He shook his head. "I don't know enough about females for that."

"Yet you claim they are artificial," she reminded him. "That pretends some knowledge."

"I am judging by the very few I met in India, and those whom I recently encountered in London," he said. "My acquaintance with them was slight, I will allow. Nevertheless, one observes certain traits. Possibly, I was unfortunate in my experiences, trivial though they were."

She considered him for a moment, a serious expression in her hazel eyes. "I think it is your attitude that is at fault, you know," she said, candidly. "You don't approach a female with the *intention* of being pleased, which is quite contrary to the practice of most gentlemen."

He laughed, despite his sombre mood. "I see," he said, in a lighter tone. "And now that you have set me right, what do you suggest I should do to overcome this most serious fault?"

She responded at once to the welcome change in him. "Why, you must undertake to approach every female with a smile, and say at least one pretty thing every ten minutes or so, while you are in her company! And if that doesn't answer, then I despair of you utterly!"

"That would be a pity," he said gravely. "Very well, ma'am. I will begin at once by saying how very charming you look today."

"Thank you. Yes, that will do for a start. Presently you must pay me another compliment. Perhaps we had better be silent now, while you rehearse one or two."

He smiled down at her. "You don't feel that such an exercise will cause my conversation to lack a certain spontaneity?"

"Why yes, possibly it will. But surely spontaneity is a small price to pay for an improved opinion of womankind?"

"If you think so."

"No, that will not do," she reproved him. "You must think so, too."

He held back the horse so that she could pass through the side gate to the Manor, which they had now reached.

"I will try to think so, since you wish it. And that is my second compliment, even if a trifle oblique," he told her.

She glanced back at him and saw that his eyes were alight with mischief. She had never seen quite that expression on his face before, although there had from time to time been occasional flashes of humour. He was becoming more mellow, she thought suddenly, los-

ing some of the sombre quality which held people at
bay. Could this change be due to her influence? She
felt a blush rising to her cheek, and quickly lowered
her eyes, annoyed with herself and perhaps just a little
with him, too.

He did not appear to notice her slight confusion, but
talked easily on general topics until they reached the
path to the stables, where they parted with a casual
goodbye. She went quickly into the house, eager to
pass on her news to Lady Chalfont; while he continued
on his way to the stables, to hand over his horse to a
recently hired groom.

As he entered the house, he noticed that the mail
was lying on the hall table. He had intended to go
straight upstairs to change out of his riding dress, but
instead he carried the letters into the Library and
glanced quickly through them. One of them was from
Chertsey; he opened that first, reading the contents
with a smile on his face. Poor old Jack, he had certainly got it badly! There was a great deal of nonsense
about Miss Langley, which Richmond skipped over
quickly, and then the information that Jack intended to
visit Chesdene in a day or two and hoped he might find
a lodging with his friend at the Manor.

"By the way," Chertsey finished, in a deplorable
scrawl that took some deciphering—"I saw your friend
Chalfont the other evening with the unspeakable
Harnby, and in the oddest company—as brutal a pair
of ruffians as I ever set eyes on, real hangman's meat,
if I'm a judge! They were all entering some filthy tavern in the Tothill fields district. How did I come to be
there myself, you'll say? Three or four of us went to a
cock fight—but I assure you there'll be no more wild
doings from now on, for with the blessed hope of
spending the rest of my life with that Sweet Angel, I
must try for a pure and saintly character myself. You
may laugh! But my wild oats are all sown, I swear it!"

Richmond smiled momentarily, but was soon frowning, lost in thought. In the light of certain knowledge
he already possessed, this bit of gossip of Jack's might

have a significance which his friend could scarcely have guessed at, when he penned it.

At length he shrugged, crossed over to a writing desk, raised the flap and prepared to put the letter away in a pigeon hole which was reserved for unanswered correspondence. Only one letter rested there already; in fact, the desk generally bore a very neat, orderly appearance in contrast to a similar one which might have been found in John Chertsey's rooms in Bruton Street.

He was just about to close the desk again, when his sharp eye alighted on a small black leather box which stood in a recess between two sets of pigeon holes. The box had previously been pushed well back into the recess, so that it was scarcely visible at a casual glance; now it was clearly in view. He snatched it up, noticing at once that there were several new scratches around the metal of the small lock, and then realised that the box was no longer locked at all.

His mouth hardened, and he set the box down to examine its contents. These were few, consisting for the most part of papers which showed the legal dealings of Christopher Richmond, Esquire, and which might well have been inspected by all the world. Nevertheless, a strong sense of outrage arose in him that any alien hand should have dared to intrude into his personal possessions. Nothing appeared to be missing; but then there was nothing of value to anyone else.

Having come to this conclusion, he lifted out the papers to uncover one or two small objects lying in the bottom of the box. Among these was a small square jewellery case. He flicked it open, and saw with a shock that its padded interior was empty.

He uttered a strong oath. The piece of jewellery which that case ought to have contained was of small intrinsic value—surely too small to tempt any professional thief in a house where objects of silver and gold were lying about?—but to Richmond it was the most valuable thing he had in his possession. He had guarded it all these years, through all manner of dangers and hardships, at times when even the few shillings it would have fetched could have brought him relief from an empty stomach. Sooner than lose it, he would have parted with his entire fortune; indeed, in losing it he had lost a vital part of himself.

Why had it been taken? He had no difficulty in guessing the answer—someone wished to know more about him. He had a shrewd idea, too, who that person was. But what use would be made of the information gained? This was the most important point of all, for it affected his own plans.

19

THE RESCUE

ON THE day following Richmond's discovery of his loss, he was astir early and left the house dressed in breeches and top boots, carrying a gun. A gardener working diligently in the overgrown shrubbery greeted him respectfully as he passed by, and ventured a remark about the weather, adding that he supposed his master was after a rabbit or two. Richmond nodded briefly.

"Pesky critturs!" said the gardener, with feeling. "Fair riddled with burrows them meadows 'long side o' the wood, an' all my young crops gettin' eaten—I've set snares, but it doesn't keep 'em down fast enough. Only place for them's the pot, y'r honour."

Richmond agreed and passed on with a quick stride which soon took him beyond the gardener's sight. He was not unobserved by other eyes, however. Sir Sidney Chalfont and Harnby stood concealed on the fringe of the wood; Harnby held a pair of perspective glasses which every now and then he would raise to his eyes and focus on the Manor.

"Richmond going shooting," said Harnby, briefly, lowering the glasses once he had ascertained who it was.

Chalfont swore roundly. "That means we'd best call it off for this morning, then. Even if Diana does decide to take a stroll in the woods, we don't want to risk Richmond butting in. What d'you say?"

Harnby was silent for a moment, evidently turning something over in his mind. Then he shook his head. "No, don't concern yourself. It may turn out even better. Thing is, I shall have to leave you in charge of operations for a while. I've just thought of something I must fetch from the King's Arms."

Chalfont protested strongly at this. He had no real liking for their scheme, to say the least, and the prospect of having to put it into operation without Harnby's guiding hand frankly unnerved him.

"For God's sake, Ferdy! It'll take you the best part of an hour to get to the King's Arms and back, even if nothing delays you there, and it's after eight already! If my cousin does decide to take a stroll in the woods today, you know as well as I do it's odds on it will be shortly after she's finished breakfast— I took trouble enough finding out about her habits, didn't I? I shall be sunk without you, and so I tell you—what's more, I wouldn't care to bet on those ruffians doing what I tell 'em! Seems to me you've more authority with 'em than I have."

"Here's a pother!" retorted Harnby, scornfully. "You sound like a maiden about to be raped, Chalfont, 'pon my soul you do! All right, all right, calm down, will you? You know exactly what to do. We've been over it all, times enough. Besides, I told you from the start that I mustn't appear on the scene at all—you must save the girl single-handed, or there's no credit in it for you. If she appears, follow the plan as we decided it. I shall be lurking somewhere in the background to get the men quickly away. But forget about that part and concentrate on the girl. And another thing—" he paused to choose his words carefully, "if anything goes slightly differently from our original plan, just act naturally. That's to say, remember that you came to see your cousin, you were told she was walking in the woods and followed her there, and you know nothing—*absolutely nothing*—about whatever should follow. It must appear to be as great a shock to you as it will be to the girl. Stick to that, and all will go smoothly. I may not turn up for some time afterwards, but don't let that concern you. I shan't be far off— trust me."

Trust was certainly not a word that sprang readily to Chalfont's mind in connection with Harnby, but he realised he had no option. He was already regretting ever having embarked on this plan, which might in the end show no return for all their trouble, not to say money. A straight gamble was one thing, but this held a different kind of hazard, and one for which he felt himself to be unfitted.

However, there was nothing left now but to go through with it; so he watched Harnby depart and settled down to his solitary vigil.

Time dragged. He stood motionless with his glasses trained on the Manor for what seemed an age. At length he lowered them and pulled out his watch from his waistcoat pocket. He looked at it and groaned. Almost an hour had gone by since Harnby had left. He felt cramped from standing so long in one position, and took a few strides up and down, careful to keep within the cover of the trees. He soon stopped, in a panic lest he should miss Diana emerging from the house. That would throw out the whole careful timing of the plan. Hastily, he took up the glasses and resumed his surveillance.

After another twenty minutes had loitered past, he began to think that the business was hopeless. Evidently she did not intend to come out at all this morning, which meant that the whole performance would need to be repeated tomorrow. He cursed aloud, suddenly recollected the need for caution, and looked furtively about him. There was no need to worry. Not a soul was about in the wood—or was there? In the silence, broken only by birdsong, he fancied he heard a twig snapping underfoot not far away, in the direction of the derelict woodman's hut where the two men were hiding. Had one of them disobeyed orders and come outside? It was possible; if so, there was no need for anxiety. They would return to cover soon enough.

With a heartfelt sigh, he raised the glasses again to survey the now detestably familiar view of the back of the house and its surrounding paths and gardens, and the lane which ran at one side of it leading eventually to the wood. After a few moments, his attention quickened. Had he detected someone crossing the lawn in the direction of the gate that gave on to the lane—someone in light-coloured garments, a female? He cursed as the object became momentarily lost to view, and switched his attention to the lane, fiddling with the sight adjustment on the glasses. If it should indeed be his cousin, she should soon emerge from the gate and stand in clear view as she turned to walk down the lane. And yes! There she was; with the aid of the glasses, he could now identify her with certainty, strolling slowly down the lane clad in a lemon-coloured gown.

He did not wait for more, but ran to the hut to alert the two men. They listened to his gabbled last minute instructions with mocking smiles which were very little to his liking.

"Ay, guv," returned one of them. "Don't 'ee fret—we knows what to do."

"Well, just see to it that you only put up a show of resistance," he flung at them, as he rushed off, "and on no account hurt the lady."

He left the shelter of the wood at the point where the lane led into it through a small wooden turnstile. Instead of going through the turnstile, however, he pushed into the undergrowth which grew thickly at one side of it, making his way for the shelter of the hedge which bordered that side of the lane. It was a wretched progress; bent nearly double, for fear of observation, he exposed his face all the time to either nettle stings or the clawing of briars. He dared not employ his stick, which he clutched in one hand for future use, to beat aside the obstacles from his path. This would have created the kind of stir which might be noticed even from a distance. He could only suffer in an eloquent silence until at last he was free of the entangling briars and bushes, and safe behind the shelter of the hedge. He paused, panting for breath, still bent almost double, for the hedge was not very high, though of a satisfactory thickness. It was a warm day; the sun was beating down on his face, sore from its recent battering. He pressed himself close against the hedge, feeling in his pocket for a clean handkerchief. Having found one, he passed it several times over his sweating face, then smoothed down his hair. He certainly would not look his usual urbane self on this occasion, but Diana would be too occupied to notice at first; afterwards, he would have the best of reasons for looking dishevelled.

His next period of trial was waiting for Diana to enter the wood. Later, he decided that this was probably worse than the earlier waiting period. If anything should go wrong now—if she should discover him lurking behind the hedge, for instance, what excuse could he offer? He began an attempt to turn over some plausible excuses, but found he was incapable of coherent thought. Everything now must depend on impulse. He could only hope fervently that it would all proceed as planned.

It seemed a lifetime before Diana reached the bottom of the lane. As she drew nearer, he could hear her humming a little, evidently pleased with herself and the morning. So much the better; in such a state of euphoria, she would be all the more vulnerable. She pushed the turnstile and stepped through into the wood. Not until she had penetrated beyond the fringes of it did he dare to move from his hiding place. Then he attempted to scramble over the hedge, having first thrown his stick over into the lane.

He quickly discovered that it is not easy to climb over an unkempt hedge: it has a disconcerting trick of yielding beneath the weight of a man's body, the better to impale him on its twigs. After several unsuccessful attempts during which his face and hands again suffered badly, he did at last manage to surmount the obstacle and land sprawling in the lane.

He staggered painfully to his feet, attempting to brush himself down so that he might appear much as usual, but he feared that it was a hopeless task. There were several rents in his clothes besides all the ravages to his face, and he simply dared not think what his cravat must look like by this time.

It was at this point that he heard a loud cry for help. Here was his cue. Picking up his stick he dashed forward, pushed through the turnstile, and went at a spanking pace into the wood. He had not gone far when he came upon the scene which he had expected.

Diana was in the grip of an evil-looking ruffian who had one hand clamped over her mouth to prevent any more cries for help. In spite of the fact that he had both her arms pinioned behind her, she was putting up a strong resistance, kicking out at his shins and trying hard to butt him with her head. Preoccupied as he was with his own part in the plan, Chalfont could not help thinking what a spirited filly she was.

Raising the stick, he rushed forward into the fray.

"Unhand that lady, you villain!" he shouted. "Let her go at once, d'you hear?"

Feigning surprise, the man released Diana and turned to face Chalfont. At the same moment, a second rough-looking character rushed out from the trees, seized Diana and put his hand over her mouth.

Unfortunately, for him, he misjudged the position slightly, leaving her upper lip free for a second. It was long enough for her to seize the chance of sinking her teeth into his forefinger. With a yelp of pain, he momentarily pulled his hand away. She promptly screamed, at the same time struggling frantically to free herself from his clutches.

Meanwhile, Chalfont was making a brave showing with the first assailant, who allowed himself to be beaten off after a few minutes of sparring, retreating a little distance to hold his head as though half stunned by the blows he had received. Chalfont then turned his attention to the other man, pulling him away from Diana with an ease which must have been suspect to an uninvolved spectator. Raising the stick once again, Chalfont laid it about the man's body in a series of blows which appeared much more violent than in fact they were.

The first man was still in the background, nursing his head. Suddenly the second one capitulated, ducking out from under the flailing stick and taking to his heels. His companion, seeing this, seemed to make a rapid recovery, for he joined the other man in headlong flight. Chalfont started after them. Everything was going according to plan, so far.

At that moment, a shot rang out.

Startled, Chalfont stopped in his tracks. This was something unexpected, something quite outside the original plan. He turned his head sharply in the direction of the sound; it had come from fairly close at hand.

Then he saw the sun glinting on the barrel of a gun protruding from a thick bush in a direct line with the spot where Diana, breathless and exhausted from her recent exertions, was standing quite still. There could be no doubt at all about it—the gun was trained on Diana.

What Chalfont did then was perhaps the one heroic action of his life. He flung himself forward, bearing Diana to the ground and shielding her body with his, just as a second shot spat towards them.

He felt a sharp, searing pain in his right arm. This, together with the bang on the head received as he made contact with the ground, made him feel muzzy.

For the moment he could do no more. Diana, too, stunned by her fall, lay motionless, partly under him.

She was senseless only for a few moments. As she came round she heard the retreating sounds of a horse galloping through the wood; then a nearer sound, that of someone trampling twigs underfoot with a hasty stride.

She stirred, trying to sit up. The movement roused Sir Sidney. He groaned and rolled away from her, clutching his right forearm where a patch of blood showed on the sleeve. Painfully he struggled to a sitting position.

At that moment, a man burst out of the trees and ran towards them.

"Good God!" he exclaimed, his face paling under the tan. "Diana! Are you hurt?"

He knelt beside them, placing his arm about Diana as if to raise her from the ground.

She pushed it away, looking first into his face with cold, accusing eyes, and then fixing her glance on the gun which he had set down hastily on the ground.

"No, I am not hurt," she said, in a voice charged with contempt in spite of its trembling. "But it's no thanks to you. You fired those shots. Which of us did you intend them for—myself or Sir Sidney?"

20

A RECKONING

HE PAID no heed to the accusation, but asked a sharp question of his own. "The shots—where did they come from?"

"I—I'm not sure—over there, I think—" Her teeth were chattering so that he could scarcely hear what she said, but she gestured towards the bush.

"That bush," collaborated Chalfont thickly, raising his head a little. "Saw the barrel pointed at Diana— must have been you, Richmond—I know why."

Richmond leapt to his feet, taking up the gun and raising it to his shoulder. "Keep down!" he ordered them.

He advanced cautiously towards the bush, taking cover from tree to tree. Although they only half believed in what he was doing, they were both too shaken to ignore any rules of possible safety, so they obeyed his injunction, watching his manoeuvres with as much attention as they could muster. He drew nearer to his objective, then fired. After waiting a few moments, he plunged into the middle of the bush, disappearing from view.

Running feet sounded from the lane, and there was a shout from someone who burst suddenly into the wood.

"Miss Diana! Dear God, ma'am, is it you? Are you hurt?"

Diana recognised with relief the agitated voice of her gardener, Jemina's husband. He ran towards them, kneeling beside her and imploring her to tell him if she was all right.

"I heard someone scream, and then shots. Good God, ma'am, whatever's been afoot?"

"I was attacked," she said, as coherently as she could, for now she was shivering violently. "I'm unhurt, but this gentleman's wounded—have a care, it may still not be safe—"

He removed his coat, placing it about her shoulders. "In our own wood, in broad daylight! Who in the world would do such a thing! Here, Miss, pull this round ye—it's not over clean, but ye're shivering with shock—small wonder! Best get ye back to the house—hullo, who's this?"

Richmond was coming back towards them. Seeing

the gun in his hand, the man started up in alarm, placing himself before his mistress.

"Ye'll not harm her, not while I'm alive to stop ye!" he growled defiantly.

"Don't be a fool, man!" Richmond laid the gun down and addressed Diana. "No one's about now, though there are plenty of signs that someone's been there. You can tell me exactly what happened later, but just now we'll get you back to the Manor." He turned to Sir Sidney. "Where are you hit, Chalfont? Can you walk if I give you a hand?"

"Damned arm," muttered Chalfont, removing his left hand, which was covered in blood, so that the other man could see the torn and bloodstained cloth on his right forearm. "Winged me—don't think the bullet's lodged there—bleeding like a pig, all the same."

"We'll try a temporary dressing," said Richmond. "Mind if I untie your cravat?" Without waiting for permission, he swiftly undid the once intricate arrangement of Sir Sidney's neckgear, and handed the strip of linen to the gardener. "Now off with your coat—"

He helped Chalfont remove the coat, taking it gingerly over the injured arm. In spite of his care, the wounded man blanched, muttering an oath.

"Sorry." Richmond rolled back the torn shirt sleeve, revealing a jagged gash from which blood poured freely. He took a clean handkerchief from his pocket and, using it as a pad, bound the cravat about Sir Sidney's arm. It was quickly and dexterously done, so that those looking on realised he was not unpractised in first aid. "You'll do till we get a medico," he pronounced, taking up his gun and offering an arm to Chalfont. He signed to the gardener to assist Diana, and the four of them made a halting progress to the house.

Little was said on the way, but Diana did manage to relate how she had first been set upon by two men before the firing began.

"Poachers, d'ye reckon, sir?" asked the gardener of Richmond, in a puzzled tone. "There's nobbut rabbits hereabouts, this time o' year, and anyone can have 'em for the takin'—proper plagued with the pesky critturs, we be, that's for sure! But who'd set on Miss Diana?"

"You may well ask," returned Richmond, then, feeling Chalfont wince, "how goes it?"

"Damnably," muttered Sir Sidney, between clenched teeth.

"We're almost there," Richmond consoled him, as the forlorn party entered the Manor gate.

They had not gone far up the drive before they were observed by one of Richmond's servants, who hastened out to see what was wrong, bringing others in his train. One was bidden to ride off for a doctor, while the two maid-servants were told to help Miss Chalfont into the house. Richmond accompanied the party to the door of the Dowager's Wing and there left them.

He returned briefly to his own quarters in order to leave his gun, then started off across the green at a smart pace for the Red Lion. At this moment, he was sorely in need of information, and Joe Astill at the Red Lion was the most reliable source he knew in the village. Moreover, anyone either approaching or leaving Chesdene was bound to pass by the village inn.

It did not take him long to discover that Joe had seen the two men who had attacked Diana.

"It was after I 'eerd them shots down in the wood, y'r honour. They comes scuttlin' across the green as if th' devil's after 'em, never stoppin' to wet their whistles at the tap—not that I want to see the likes o' them in my 'ouse—an' makin' sraight for the coach road. Matter o'—" Joe paused to scratch his head—"say, half an hour or so agone, Sir. Not the first time I've seed 'em hereabouts lately, neither, but I 'opes as it'll be the last."

"When did you see them before?"

"First thing this mornin', for onct. A carter from the town dropped 'em just outside 'ere. And another time, a day or two back—an' ye'll not believe, y'r honour, whose company they was in. None other—" the land-lord leaned confidentially over his counter, although

there was no one but Richmond in the taproom—
"none other than the new baronet up at the Manor!
There was another gentleman with 'im, too, but who he
was, I can't say, never 'aving set eyes on 'im afore
though I've seen 'im since. A portly gentleman, 'e was,
with rather a 'igh colour, as though 'e might go off in a
'plexy one of these days." He shook his head know-
ingly.

"I think I know who you mean. When did you see
him again? Today, by any chance?"

The landlord nodded. "Ay, y'r honour. Twice—
onct first thing this morning, soon after them gallows
birds gets down from the cart and goes along the road
leadin' round the wood. 'Im—'plexy gennelman, I
means, sir—an' Sir Sidney Chalfont comes together on
'horseback, an' leaves their nags 'ere, y'r honour, then
goes across the green towards the Manor, an' out o'
sight for a bit. T'would be about an hour later, give or
take a bit, that I sees 'plexy gent comin' back. Takes 'is
nag 'e does, in a devil of a 'urry, an' rides off for the
coach road. Thinks I, what's amiss? but there seems no
way o' knowing, not till I sees the servants from the
Manor later on in the day, an' till then I must bide m'
time. So I gets on wi' my work, an' about an hour
later, when I've nigh forgotten all about 'im, back
comes 'plexy gent at the gallop, goes straight past an'
down the road goin' round the wood. Hearin' a nag at
the gallop, I rushes out into the yard, an' just sees 'im
as 'e goes past."

"I want you to think carefully, Astill," said Richmond, in quiet, authoritative tones. "Had this gentleman anything with him when he returned which he was
not carrying when he went?"

"Funny ye should mention that, y'r honour, for I
noticed that partikleer. He was carryin' a gun when 'e
comes back again."

"Ah!" Richmond let out a long-drawn sigh of satisfaction, then felt in his pocket and produced a coin.
"You're a very observant man, Astill, and are wasting
your talents here in Chesdene. I feel you should be

writing reports for one of the London journals. But talking's thirsty work, so draw yourself a tankard."

He slapped the coin down on the counter and, leaving the Red Lion, hastened towards the Manor.

As he approached the house, he saw that a smart curricle with yellow wheels stood outside the entrance. A gentleman in fawn pantaloons and a dark blue coat of Melton cloth with large silver buttons, was standing on the step in conversation with the butler. Richmond recognised the visitor at once, and hailed him.

"Jack! You're the very person I most wished to see at present!"

Chertsey turned with his ready smile. "Well, here I am, Kit, just as I said I'd be!" Then, seeing the expression on his friend's face—"Nothing wrong, is there, old fellow?"

"Tight corner," murmured Richmond in his ear. "Need your help." Aloud, he said, "Come with me round to the stables, and leave Poulton to see to your baggage."

Chertsey asked no questions, but followed him at once; they had been in tight corners enough together out in the East. Until they were both mounted and riding across the green in the direction of the coach road, Richmond made no attempt to explain. Once past the Red Lion, where Joe Astill took note of them, he told Chertsey what he had suspected had taken place that morning in the wood.

"But how can you be sure?" asked the other, puzzled. "Even if the landlord did see him with a gun, what the devil could he stand to gain by trying to kill Miss Chalfont? I can see the point of the rescue scheme, of course—just such an addlepated notion as that ass Chalfont would think up! But there seems no motive—and, anyway, you've no clear proof that Harnby did in fact fire the gun."

"There's a strong enough motive, believe me, Jack, but I haven't time now to explain it to you. There ahead of us, if I mistake not, are two fellows who can help clear up a part of the mystery. We're going to grab them, Jack, so be ready."

Ahead of them were two men walking along the road at a spanking pace. They drew well into the hedge as the riders passed them, looking up for a moment with a wary expression on their unprepossessing faces. Richmond and Chertsey rode on a little farther, until they came to a bend in the road. Here they dismounted, tethering their horses to a field gate and taking cover behind a hawthorn tree which grew close to the bend.

What followed was expertly done, and all over in a matter of minutes. The men were not expecting any trouble, which undoubtedly made matters easier.

"What ye want wi' us?" one of them croaked, as he struggled to break the stranglehold being applied by Richmond. "Done ye' no 'arm—never set eyes on ye afore!"

"You attacked a lady in the wood at Chesdene and all but murdered her, you dog!" Richmond emphasised his point by applying further pressure to his captive's neck.

The man could do nothing but gurgle, but his companion was more articulate, in spite of Chertsey's ungentle grasp. In colourful Cockney not always easy to follow, he gave his captors to understand that there had never been the slightest intention of harming the lady, the object of the exercise being to put up an appearance of danger so that she might be rescued by the 'Swell', as he termed Chalfont. "Never 'urt an 'air of 'er 'ead," he ended, virtuously.

"Just as well for you," returned Richmond. "Well, it's as I thought, Jack! All right, you two, if you answer all my questions truthfully, I might consider—might, I say—letting you go. But I want the truth, mind, and if I don't think I'm getting it, we'll haul you before the Justice and see whether he can loosen your tongues for you."

He released his captive, and the man was then able to join his confederate in swearing, though somewhat hoarsely, to tell the truth, the whole truth and nothing but the truth.

"Very likely," said Richmond, dryly. "But it won't pay you to do otherwise, as you could face a charge of attempted murder."

At this, they broke into terrified protests which Richmond swept aside.

"Someone fired two shots," he reminded them grimly. "Was that part of the original plan?"

"No, it weren't, y'r honour, an' that's when we scarpered. Barkers is one fing we don't 'ave nuffink to do wi', me an' me mate 'ere. I says to 'im, I says—"

"Two more questions," cut in Richmond. "First—do you know why the plan was changed, and a gun introduced?"

The men looked at each other and shook their heads. All they knew, they said, was that the Fat Swell had gone off suddenly, leaving the other one in charge, and was absent some time.

"But I seen 'im come back," said one of them, "creepin' along quiet like, an' a-carryin' this barker, just afore we rushes out to scare the moll, like we bin told by t'other Swell—"

"You're quite sure of that?" asked Richmond sharply. "That you saw Harnby—the other man, that's to say—with a gun? Think well before you answer, because there are ways of finding out if you're lying."

The man swore once again that every word he was uttering was gospel. Richmond nodded, knowing full well that this part of their story was corroborated by Joe Astill at the Red Lion.

"But you didn't see him fire it?" he went on.

"Not to say see'd 'im, y'r honour, but it was 'im, right enough. An' when we 'ears that shot, me an' me mate, we scarpers off straightway—no one tells us anyfink about barkers, and barkers is one thing we don't 'old with, see? So off we goes, 'im 'avin' paid us somefink on account, an' us reckonin' best not to 'ang around for the rest, seeing as things looked like takin' a nasty turn all at once."

"Very wise," said Richmond, dryly. "And I hope you'll continue to behave as wisely for the future. I'm going to let you two go, for now, but I'd advise you to lose no time in taking yourselves out of this parish and back to whatever hole you crawled out of. I intend to furnish the parish constable with your description, and if you should come anywhere within his reach, you'll certainly regret it. So, on your way."

The men needed no second bidding, but started off at a run down the road. When Richmond and Chertsey rode past them a few minutes later, they were still running hard.

"They'll burst their lungs!" said Chertsey, with a laugh. "And no loss to anyone. But should we have turned them loose, Kit?"

"Perhaps not, though they were only taking part in a play, after all. But I have a particular reason for wishing to manage this affair as quietly as possible—a personal reason. I haven't told you the whole story by a long way, Jack, but I'll do so now, as we go along to collect Harnby—I hope. I scarcely think he'll have had time yet to leave the King's Arms for London, or wherever it is he had it in mind to go; but all the same, we'll put on speed. I wouldn't miss an interview with that gentleman for the half of my fortune."

Looking at his friend's expression, Chertsey could believe his words. They both set their horses at the gallop; and, as the miles dwindled before them, Richmond told his story. At the end of it, Chertsey nodded.

"So that's how it was. Well, I always knew there was something in your past you preferred to keep to yourself, and there had to be a good reason for your sudden decision to return to England. But all this puts Chalfont in a bit of a fix, don't it?"

Richmond's face darkened. "Nothing to the fix I'd like to put him in, the swine! But the real villain of the piece is Harnby—I'm looking forward to my encounter with him."

"If he hasn't shown us a clean pair of heels," said Chertsey.

This had the effect of making Richmond press his horse still harder, and in a very short time they turned into the archway of the King's Arms.

They were just in time to witness the luggage being fastened on to a post chaise which stood ready in the yard. As they watched, the passenger came out of the inn towards the vehicle and prepared to mount the steps.

Richmond dismounted from his horse, whistling to an ostler to take it from him. He strolled over to the passenger, who turned an apprehensive face towards him.

"Don't put yourself to the trouble of entering this chaise, Harnby," said Richmond, almost pleasantly. "You're not going anywhere at present, I regret to say."

21

THE MAN KNOWN AS RICHMOND

SOME HOURS later, both Diana and Sir Sidney were feeling a good deal recovered. The latter's arm had been given proper medical attention and was now supported by a sling; a few glasses of excellent brandy, sent in by Richmond's orders from his well-chosen cellar, had restored the colour to Chalfont's countenance and a little more of his customary confidence to his manner. He was seated in a comfortable wing chair in Lady Chalfont's sunny parlour, reflecting that perhaps things had not turned out so badly, after all. There could be no doubt that he had saved his kinswoman at least from severe injury, if not from death. She evidently understood this herself, for at present she was engaged in thanking him. They were alone in the room, as Lady Chalfont had been so alarmed by the whole affair that the doctor had given her a sedative and recommended that she should lie down on her bed for a few hours. She had tried vainly to persuade her daughter to do the same, but Diana's excellent constitution was more than equal even to an upset of this nature; besides, there were several things which puzzled her, and she needed to talk them over with someone.

"But for your prompt action, who knows what might have happened?" she asked, in concluding her thanks. "Can you be positive, though, cousin, that the shots were indeed intended for me, and not for yourself?"

"There can't be a doubt of it. The gun was pointed in your direction. I saw it plainly—that was why I sprang forward."

She hesitated for a few moments, then said, in a tone of suppressed emotion, "Do you really think—is it possible that Mr. Richmond was responsible? I must confess I jumped to that conclusion at first; but then his actions afterwards were not those, surely, of a man who has just attempted to kill someone. No one could be so—so—"

"Cold blooded?" queried Chalfont, grimly. "I'd not put it past him. He's a cool customer, I'll wager. Besides, he has a very good reason—or thinks he has, which comes to the same thing—for doing you a mischief. He's got a grudge against your family."

"A grudge?" She looked at him incredulously. "How could he have? I never saw him before the day he came to offer himself as a tenant here."

"That's all you know," Chalfont said meaningly. "I've something here, if I can get at it—"

He broke off, trying to reach an inside pocket in his coat. Diana watched his fumblings with what patience she could muster, until at last she was forced to offer her help. He accepted gratefully and under his guidance she drew out a pocket book from which she extracted a small object enclosed in a protective pocket of soft felt.

"Take it out of the case," he instructed, "and examine it carefully."

She did as he bid. The object disclosed was a beautifully chased gold locket, a little too large for her taste, on a chain. For a moment, she mistook his intention and feared that he was about to make her a present of it. She started to thrust it back into its case, but he stopped her with a shake of his head.

"No. I want you to examine it."

Puzzled now, she took the locket into her hand, turning it over. Finding nothing remarkable on the outside except the beauty of the workmanship, at last she opened it. She had some difficulty, as the clasp was stiff, but presently it yielded to display a tiny portrait on each side. One was of a young girl with black curls and lively dark eyes; she reminded Diana of someone, but she could not for the moment think who it was. On the other side was the portrait of a young man with light brown hair, an aquiline nose and blue eyes—very like a portrait Diana possessed of her father.

She stared at the pictures for a while in silence, then noticed that there was some writing round their lower edge. She raised the locket nearer to her eyes, for the writing was minute and somewhat faded. Under the portrait of the girl was written 'Amelia Broughton'. She frowned, and studied the other. It was 'Ralph Chalfont'.

She looked up from the locket, her eyes searching Sir Sidney's face. "What is it? Where did you get it?"

"It's a portrait of your father's younger brother, and the girl he married," Chalfont replied. "As for whose it is, it belongs to the man you know as Richmond."

"The man I know—!" She was dumbfounded at first, then light seemed to break on her. "Oh! He has been restoring the house to what it was formerly, and I suppose he has turned this up somewhere, among all the pictures and objets d'art that he's managed to track down. But how could such a thing have come to be sold, in the first place? I am sure neither Mama nor Papa would consent to parting with a family possession such as this—why, it must have belonged to my Aunt Amelia, all those years ago!"

"You're quite right there. It did belong to your Aunt Amelia. And now it belongs to her son—the man you know as Richmond, who tried to kill you today because he swore long ago to get even with your family for all his mother suffered at their hands."

She stared at him as if she thought he had taken leave of his senses. Then her gaze dropped to the locket which she still held open in her hand. The dead Amelia's once dark, laughing eyes looked up at her, and suddenly she realised why that face had seemed familiar. It strongly resembled Christopher Richmond.

"No!" she exclaimed, involuntarily, and the hand that held the locket trembled.

Chalfont could not help feeling some satisfaction at her evident distress, as it enabled him to assume the role of protector. It was rarely that his kinswoman showed any signs of needing one.

"Can't be any doubt of it," he said, rising and going to her chair to bend over her in a comforting attitude. "Don't be alarmed, my dear Diana— I'll not let him harm you. Now that we've rumbled his little game, he'll not dare to make any more attempts on your life, in any case," he added; as an afterthought which detracted somewhat from his previous assurance, had he but stopped to consider it.

"I—I just can't believe it," she stammered, brokenly. "I thought—he seemed—oh!"

She buried her face in her hands, letting the locket drop into her lap unheeded.

He placed his uninjured arm about her shoulders. "There, my dear girl, don't take on so! Only give me the right to protect you, and no one will be able to harm you any more!"

For a brief moment she yielded against his encircling arm, seeming to take the comfort it offered. He was about to push his luck further and drop a chaste kiss on her brow, when there came a knock on the parlour door and the housemaid poked her head inside the room. Chalfont started back hastily, cursing under his breath.

"Beg pardon, Miss, but the gentleman from next door's here again, and askin' to see you."

Diana looked up, blinking to clear the tears from her eyes. "Do you mean—Mr. Richmond?" she asked, in an unsteady voice.

The maid assented.

"Tell him I can't see him— I don't wish to see anyone at present," said Diana, striving to control her voice.

"Well, if that don't beat all!" exclaimed Chalfont, as the maid withdrew. "I'll say this, he's got nerve, that fellow!"

"And he's not the only one," retorted Richmond, flinging wide the door and striding unceremoniously into the room.

He closed the door firmly behind him, then came over to the chair where Diana was sitting. She half started up, causing the locket to slip from her lap to the floor. He looked down, saw what it was and stooped to gather it into his hand.

"Mine, I think. It's been missing for some days, but I rather guessed where it must have gone, particularly when I was informed by my staff that a portly gentleman had called to see me when I was out, and waited some time in the hope of my return. A very gifted man, your friend Harnby, it appears—he'd have made a creditable burglar."

"I make no apology for the methods I had to use," blustered Chalfont, reddening a trifle. "I felt it my duty as head of the household to try and find out just what manner of man Diana had accepted as a tenant—and how right I was, she must now see!"

Richmond's glance swerved to Diana, who was sitting rigidly in her chair in complete silence. His eyes softened.

"Does she? I wonder." He turned back to Chalfont.

"But the discovery must have come as something of a shock to you, Chalfont. By it, you lost a title and Chesdene Manor—for what that's worth."

Diana spoke for the first time, somewhat hoarsely. "Then it *is* true? There can't be any mistake—you are Robert Chalfont?"

He nodded. "Yes. Though I haven't been called by that name for almost fourteen years. I renounced it on the day I ran away from my Grandfather's house—" his mouth twisted ironically—"now mine, strange to say. But that's another story. There is a more immediate one which I fancy Miss Chalfont should hear. I think you know what I mean, Chalfont."

Chalfont had straightened up, meeting Richmond's mocking gaze aggressively. "She knows all she needs to know—that you tried to murder her! By God, Richmond, I've a mind to set the law on you, but for dragging the family's name through the mud! Don't think you can try it again, though—I've sent to Town for Dally to come straight here, and I shall acquaint him with the whole! Once the lawyer's in the know, even you won't have the audacity to make any more attempts on Diana's life."

"How very wise of you, my dear cousin-by-remove. Mr. Dally certainly is the most suitable repository for the family secrets, and it's not at all his fault that occasionally they leak out because he has been a trifle unwise in his choice of underlings, shall we say?" He looked sharply at Chalfont and saw him change colour. "But are you so very certain that you'll be able to give him accurate information about this affair? Do you in fact know the whole truth about it yourself?"

"What d'ye mean? If this is one of your tricks—"

"You're the trickster, not I. You practised a trick on Miss Chalfont to serve your own ends—"

"What trick?" asked Diana. So far, her mind had been in a turmoil which prevented her from taking any part in the conversation; now rational thought was returning, and it prompted several questions.

"Your kinsman will tell you about that himself

presently," Richmond assured her, turning aside from Chalfont for a moment. "But," he went on, addressing the other man again, "it does not seem to have occurred to you that your delightful friend Harnby might have decided to improve on the trick."

Chalfont stared at him in silence for a few moments, thunderstruck. Then he reddened angrily.

"This is another of your crafty schemes," he said, in mounting tones. "If you're trying to put the blame on Harnby for what *you* did—".

"Keep your voice down," Richmond recommended him, sharply. "The servants have enough food for gossip as it is. Like you, I am unwilling to drag the family name in the mud, little cause as I have to revere it." He paused. "Cast your mind back to this morning. You and Harnby were in the wood together, early, when I went out with a gun—it's no use to protest, I have proof of it. You saw me, and took note of the firearm. It was then, wasn't it, that Harnby suddenly decided to leave you and go back to the King's Arms? At that precise moment—moreover, he didn't tell you why. But I can tell you. Possibly—" with a shrewd glance at Chalfont's face, on which horrified comprehension was slowly dawning—"possibly you don't need telling. I can see you're beginning to understand."

"It's impossible!" exclaimed Chalfont, hoarsely. "Why should he do such a damned silly thing? Oh, yes, I can see that he might have thought it simpler to get rid of her, in the beginning, before we knew about you, that is—although I never credited him with being such a fiend as that, 'fore God, I didn't! But after we found out who you were, there would be no point in it—all the money would go to you, as heir to the Manor!"

Diana turned a bewildered look on both of them. "What is all this about? I can't make head nor tail of it! For pity's sake, tell me!"

"All in good time," replied Richmond, in a gentler tone than he had been using so far. "I have first to show our kinsman here how he has been duped by his fellow conspirator." He resumed his conversation with

Chalfont. "There's one point you've overlooked, but Harnby saw it at once. The story of how I ran away at the age of sixteen swearing revenge on the Chalfonts was known to the rest of the family. Harnby knew it, because you told him. He also knew that there were witnesses to the fact that I'd gone out with a gun that morning. If Miss Chalfont were to be killed by a shot, circumstantial evidence would arraign me as her murderer. That would get rid of both of us, wouldn't it, and leave the field clear for you? You owed him a good deal of money and he needed it pretty badly. This was the best way of making sure of it."

"My God!" said Chalfont, weakly, feeling his way to a chair and collapsing into it. "But this is all surmise—how do I know you're not just making up this tale to cover your own misdeeds?" he continued after a few minutes, rallying a little. "I shall see Harnby myself, and ask him—"

Richmond shook his head mockingly. "I fear not, Mr. Harnby has left us for a long time. An unaccountable urge came over him to explore distant lands, brought on, I believe, by an interview with Chertsey and myself an hour or so back. He did not even stay to collect the debt you owe him—by the way, I doubt if he'll ever bother to do so, which gives you one worry the less. However, he did confide the whole story to us, and it happened just as I say. Doubtless you think me an unreliable witness, in view of your recent suspicions of me. I refer you, therefore, to Chertsey, who is at this moment waiting in my own quarters here; and also to the landlord of the Red Lion, who saw Harnby on his way back from the King's Arms, carrying a gun. There were two other witnesses—the men you engaged to help you practise your comparatively harmless trick on Miss Chalfont—but they also realised that they had urgent business elsewhere. No doubt, though, they may be found eventually in the same place where you originally met them—that is, until their career ends untimely on the gallows, which I foresee it will. Have I said enough to satisfy you, now?"

All Chalfont could answer for some time was a deeply felt "Oh, my God!"

Diana broke in, almost beside herself with impatience. "For pity's sake," she implored, "tell me what all this is about! I declare I shall lose my sanity if I have to listen to any more without knowing what it means! I collect that Sir Sidney—"

"Not *Sir* Sidney," Richmond reminded her, gently. "Just plain Sidney, I fear."

"Oh, well!" she replied, impatiently. "It seems he played a trick on me—do you mean that the attack in the woods was feigned? I thought at the time that those two ruffians weren't putting up much resistance, but I forgot about that afterwards, in the stress of what followed." She turned on Chalfont accusingly. "Was that it? If so, I think it was an odious thing to do! I *was* frightened, even if the danger was not real, and had I been of a more timid disposition, it might have affected me seriously. I suppose," she finished, scornfully, "your object was to cut a heroic figure in my eyes."

"You don't understand," stuttered Chalfont. "I had to do it—I was desperate—I owed Harnby money and he was pressing me—it was all his idea, curse him—I swear before God, Diana, I never meant to harm a hair of your head! And after all's said, I did save you from serious injury—you said so yourself, remember."

Her look softened. "Yes," she admitted. "You did, and for that I must forgive the rest. But why?" she finished, with a puzzled frown. "Your object was to persuade me to marry you, but for the life of me I cannot see how that would have benefited you in any way. You speak as if your marriage to me would have enabled you to pay off your debts, but that is nonsense, as we both know! I am no heiress!"

"Oh, but you are," interposed Richmond, smiling. "Your grandfather left a considerable sum of money in trust for you, to be handed over when you attained the age of one and twenty. In the event of your death before that date, it was to revert to the heir of the estate. No one knew of this arrangement but the family lawyer, and he was sworn never to divulge it, even to yourself, until the appointed time. But Dally had a man in his employ who made it his business to make money out of such secrets. He sold it to your kinsman, here, who then saw that the best way out of his difficulties was to marry you. Harnby, however, was dissatisfied with the progress made by Chalfont in this direction, and decided to make sure of the inheritance for his protegé, by disposing of the two people who had a stronger claim to it. That is the story in a nutshell— and a very pretty tale of deception and treachery on all sides it is, you must agree."

Diana made no answer for a time, trying to take in the amazing information which had just been given her. At length she turned on Chalfont scornfully. "Fortune hunters are always despicable, even when everyone knows what they are about; but someone who tries to catch a fortune before its owner is aware that she possesses it, must be the lowest of even that low species! You needn't imagine, though, that you did succeed in taking me in—I always knew there was some ulterior motive behind your declarations of affection—"

"Believe me, Diana," Chalfont cut in, with an ingratiating smile, "it was not all feigned. Oh, yes, I'll admit I was in a tight corner, and needed to marry money but there was no one I'd rather it had been than you. I really am extremely attached to you, my dear."

"Enough of that!" said Richmond, with a snap, before Diana had time to answer this. "Your protestations can only be an insult to Miss Chalfont after what has passed! In fact, I don't think she requires your presence here any longer. She knows all now, and can have nothing further to say to you. I'll have my carriage sent round to convey you to the King's Arms, and from there you may go to the devil for all I care. Be good enough to ring for the housemaid, ma'am, and I'll give her the message."

As Diana did so, she reflected that Richmond's methods were perhaps a trifle high-handed; surely it was for her to send Sidney Chalfont away? Instead of resenting his action, however, she realised she actually welcomed it. It was an unaccustomed luxury to have someone else making the decisions, and at present she certainly did want to be rid of her despicable kinsman.

"One thing, Chalfont," said Richmond, when he had given the maid his instructions and was awaiting the other man's departure, "I can't forget that you did in fact save my cousin's life. Whatever else you've done, that must stand to your credit. If you like to let me have an account of your present debts, therefore, I'll see that they're settled. Don't run away with the notion, though, that I shall be prepared to haul you out everytime you choose to get into deep water. This present relief is all I ever intend to offer. Visiting debtors' prisons is decidedly not in my line, so if you should find yourself inside one any time in the future, you are likely to stay there as far as I'm concerned. Bear that in mind."

22

THE TENANT TAKES POSSESSION

AFTER SIDNEY CHALFONT had gone, there was an uneasy silence between the other two for some moments.

"I suppose," said Richmond, at last, "that you would like me to go, too, so that you can have some time to yourself to straighten matters out in your own mind? All that you've just learnt must have come as something of a shock, to say the least."

"Oh, yes—but pray don't go yet! There's so much I

still don't understand—so many questions I need to ask—"

"Ask away," he replied, smiling, as he took a chair close to hers.

"Where on earth shall I begin? I don't know—how did you find out about my inheritance, for one thing?"

"I may not inherit the long nose of the Chalfonts, but I do have my fair share of curiosity," he answered, in a light tone. "Curiosity took me to a gaming club frequented by Chalfont. I wanted to see what kind of man it was who was supposed to have inherited Chesdene. Our kinsman left the club in the small hours, slightly the worse for liquor, and was accosted by a man who insisted that he wanted to see Chalfont on a matter of business, something to Chalfont's advantage. Chalfont thought he was a footpad, and enlisted the aid of Chertsey and myself, who were nearby, in driving him off. It was all rather amusing really," he broke off to comment, laughing softly at the recollection.

"No doubt, but I wish you will tell me the point of it," she said, impatiently. "Who was the man—anyone who matters?"

"Our friend Collins, from your lawyer's office—who else?"

"Oh, I see! And he wanted to tell Sidney Chalfont about my inheritance? But how did you discover that?"

"Well, it occurred to me that anything which it was to Chalfont's advantage to know from that source, might also interest me. I decided to keep my eyes and ears open. And very soon, I noticed—who could help it?—Chalfont's gallantry towards you, and I was given to understand by everyone who knew you well that it was in marked contrast to his relations with you up to that time." He paused. "That in itself meant nothing—the fellow might have fallen in love with you. What was more likely?"

"In love with me!" scoffed Diana, ignoring the final remark, though she noted it. "He never once deceived me on that score! It was all so obviously feigned, I wonder he thought to take me in!"

"So I learnt from Jack, who had it from your friend Miss Langley. I found Jack an invaluable source of information on your opinions and tastes, by the way, because the poor fellow could never lose the opportunity of repeating to me almost verbatim every conversation he had with your friend."

Diana smiled. "How absurd! But I'm so glad they're to make a match of it. I think they will suit admirably."

"So do I. Jack is the best of good fellows, and she seems a sweet, compliant girl."

"Unlike myself," laughed Diana. "I fear I'm not at all compliant!"

"Possibly," he said, letting his dark eyes rest for a moment on her face, "it will not be a virtue sought after by your future husband, whoever he may be."

"Oh, nobody, I should imagine!" she said, turning away from his gaze. "I always said I was cut out for an old maid."

"The pattern has changed, then, since I was last in England," he replied, with mock gravity.

"Never mind that, now! There's no time for nonsense—I've still a thousand questions to ask! So you pretty soon guessed what the clerk had told my kinsman. But how did you manage to confirm it—how did you come to know for certain?"

"I decided that Collins, the clerk, would repay a little investigation. Having turned up several shady incidents in his past professional life, I made a bargain with him—the information he'd passed on to Chalfont in exchange for a few days to get clear before I informed his employer of his misdeeds. He told me what I wanted to know."

"Ought you to have done that?" she asked, doubtfully. "Shouldn't he have been brought to justice?"

"What justice? His job is gone, and as Dally certainly won't give him a character, he's unlikely to obtain another half as good elsewhere. Rough justice, perhaps, but still justice enough, to my way of thinking."

"Yes," she said thoughtfully, considering him. "You know, I fancy I wouldn't care to cross swords with you. You are not ruthless, precisely, but you deal with your enemies in a frighteningly efficient manner."

He shrugged. "Experience has taught me that there can be no shilly-shallying with a rogue. But you have nothing to fear—*we* are not likely to be at outs in anything."

"Yet once you swore to be avenged on all the Chalfonts," she reminded him.

His brow darkened. "I was a boy then, and had been taunted beyond endurance at a time when I had lost the only creature I loved in the world. Time works its changes on us."

"Tell me what befell you after you ran away from the Manor," she said, leaning forward in her chair and fixing her clear eyes on his face. "I only know that they said you boarded a ship that was lost with all hands in the Bay of Biscay, and you were believed drowned with the others."

"It is a miracle that I wasn't. Mercifully, I remember very little now of that dreadful ordeal; but I was picked up by an East Indiaman bound for Bombay. I was the sole survivor of the wreck. Being young and healthy, I soon recovered and was able to make myself useful on board. The Captain could see that I was no rough seafaring lad, and he questioned me about my origins. At first, I tried to head him off; but, having won his promise that he would not try to return me to my family, I confided my name and story to him. I did not know this for some years afterwards, but at the time he set it all down, and lodged the writing with a lawyer when he returned to England. He did this so that I should have attested proof of my identity if ever there should be any question of an inheritance. Other than that the only proof I possessed was my mother's locket, which I fastened round my neck before I quitted the Manor for good, and which I was still wearing when they picked me up from the sea."

"The locket which betrayed your identity to Sidney Chalfont, and which he showed to me? From what was said, I collect that it was stolen from your rooms by that odious man Harnby."

He nodded. "That reckoning is paid, though not in full. It should have been a heavier one—I can't forget he attempted your life. Had not Chertsey been there to prevent it, I believe I might have made an end of him."

She shivered at his look. "Thank heaven you did not! It might have meant another period of exile for you, and he isn't worth it. But perhaps," she went on, glad to change the subject, "you didn't regard your time in the Indies as an exile. How did you fare when you landed there, as a young boy? How did you find a livelihood?"

"The Captain of the ship which rescued me found me some menial work with a trader at first. When I left home, I had decided to change my name— I wanted no more of Chalfont!—so I chose Christopher Richmond because my father's second name was Christopher, and also because the initials of it were my own in reverse. As Richmond I lived in India, never disclosing my real identity to anyone save Captain Orford—even when I became such firm friends with Chertsey, I didn't confide in him, though I was often tempted to do so. I suppose by that time the habit of reticence about my origins had grown on me."

"And as the years passed, you did well for yourself, I suppose, since Mr. Chertsey says you are prodigiously wealthy?" she asked, with a smile.

"Later—much later. At first, there were many hardships, but I'll not weary you with those. After some years, I obtained a post in the East India Company, and that's when I met Jack. We saw some action together, for there were frequent wars among the native States, and we proved the strength of each other's friendship in those days. As time went on, our affairs prospered, until Jack decided to return home and look about him for a wife. It was the first time we had been separated by so great a distance for many years."

"You must have missed him sadly," she said, in a gentle tone. "Was it that which decided you to return to England yourself? It couldn't have been the advertisements for news of Robert Chalfont which brought you, for they were inserted in the journals almost two years since."

"They were brought to my notice by Captain Orford. He has never completely lost touch with me, although for some years now he's been living retired at Plymouth. I knew more than a year ago that I might return and claim Chesdene Manor and the baronetcy, if I chose. Even though Jack was going home, it has taken me all this time to make up my mind on the issue."

"Why? Were you happy there?"

"Happy!" For a moment, a bitterness returned to his tone. "Who can claim to be happy? I certainly have never expected so much. I was—reasonably satisfied with my lot, I suppose."

"Yet you did decide to return, in the end. I wonder why? And why did you conceal your identity from me and from Mr. Dally, and offer yourself as a tenant for what was your own house? Oh, dear," she said, ruefully, breaking off, "I do seem to be asking an awful lot of questions! I'm sure you must think it very impertinent in me."

"No," he replied, with a shake of the head. "I want you to understand me better, and you are a member of my family, after all—although I don't think of you as a cousin, and have no wish to do so," he added, somewhat obscurely. "But to explain all this to you means I must bring to the light of day feelings which have lain hidden for many years. I'm not sure—" there was suppressed emotion in his tone—"that it isn't wiser to let them rest in peace."

"No," she said impulsively stretching out her hand towards him. "You are not at peace while they remain hidden. Tell me."

He took her hand, holding it in both his while he looked into her eyes with an intense expression on his face.

"No, Diana, I am not, and in some ways I don't deserve to be. For I did nurse feelings of revenge for many years—feelings which sprang up afresh when I learnt that I was heir to Chesdene. For a time, I had a wild fancy to return—I confess it freely to you now, and you must judge me for it as you will—and to make such a life for you and your mother as my own mother had once known, under the cruel tyranny of our grandfather."

She took a deep breath. "Who can blame you?" she said, with difficulty. "Even I, who cannot remember my Aunt Amelia, can feel indignation whenever I am put in mind of what she was made to suffer."

For a time, he could not trust himself to speak, but held her hand tightly, gazing at her with eyes that seemed to look far beyond her to scenes in which she had no part. She felt a sudden urge to throw her arms about him and clasp him to the comfort of her breast, the hurt child that was now a man strong enough to fight off every enemy except his memories.

"And there's something else which you may not realise," he continued, in a faraway voice. "I loved every stick and stone of the Manor—I never ceased to see it in my inward eye, whatever my outward surroundings might be. This countryside, too, our beautiful English countryside, was always in my thoughts amid the heat, dust and dirt of India. That day when I rode down the lanes, returning to Chesdene after so many years, the sight of it all was like a fever in my blood—no one can possibly understand who has not, like myself, been an exile for so long."

He paused, drew a long breath, and seemed to return from the distance that had claimed him. "So you see," he continued in a more matter-of-fact tone, "although I tried to forget about my inheritance, in the end those two inducements brought me back, a love of Chesdene and hatred of the Chalfonts. But I was not the idealistic boy I had been when I left Chesdene, and I wanted to see if the place still meant anything to me, or if I had just been nurturing a dream all those years. I also wanted to meet my Aunt and yourself, and the man who had inherited my estate. Until I had done this, I determined to make no move to claim Chesdene—after all, when I saw it again, it might mean less than nothing to me."

She drew her hand gently away from his.

"It must have been a very sad thing for you to see your once lovely home so neglected," she said softly. "Did you find that all its appeal was gone as a result?"

He shook his head emphatically. "From the moment I saw the chimneys of the Manor on the skyline as I rode down into the village, I knew that the old magic was still at work. Its dilapidation only served to increase my anger—forgive me, I feel it now no longer—for your father, and through him, for yourself."

"What could I have done?" she asked, with a catch in her voice. "As for Papa, I know—"

He caught her hand again. "The past is dead, Diana. I have buried my hate at last. When I saw you that day, in the church where our ancestors are remembered, I guessed at once who you must be. Physically, at any rate, you are a Chalfont, and the sight of you brought all my bitterest feelings to the surface. But later, when I called at the Manor as a prospective tenant, those feelings began to recede. It was not only that you were—are—beautiful and charming, enough to turn any man's head—it was your courageousness, your determination to make the best of a bad situation." He broke off and smiled tenderly. "The way you showed me all the points of this lamentable house! I was in no mood for laughter when I arrived, but very soon I was hard put to it to keep a straight face, I can tell you!"

She gave a little self-conscious laugh and tried to draw her hand from his grasp, but he would not permit it. "I suppose I did cut rather a ridiculous figure," she admitted, ruefully. "But how was I to know that I was showing round someone who knew far more about the Manor than I did myself?"

"A ridiculous figure? No such thing. If I smiled, it is as one smiles when one's feelings are deeply touched—your courage, your determination and optimism in the face of all your difficulties, could not fail to move me. And before many more weeks had gone by, I realised that your situation was not so dissimilar to hers—to my mother's. You had both been badly treated by those whose business it should have been to safeguard you. No, I *will* say this now—" as she dragged her hand away and a spark of anger showed in her eyes—"although I promised never to refer to the subject again. I will respect your loyalty to your father's memory, while reserving the right to think of his actions as I must. But what really matters is that at last I have come to terms with the past. My bitterness has burnt itself out, and I am ready to go forward into the future with happier feelings."

The anger had left her eyes and was replaced by a softer look. "I am so glad," she said, quietly. "Believe me, I always felt so deeply for that poor boy, every time anyone mentioned his name! I could so well understand what he must have suffered. Sometimes I have thought—I know it is absurd!—that I wished I could go back in time, as I am now, and offer him comfort—"

"You can't go back in time, Diana—and I don't wish you to, believe me!—but you can offer comfort to the man whom the boy has become. Will you?"

A quick blush came to her cheek, and she moved back in her chair, away from him. "Oh, you have no need of comfort now," she said, trying to speak lightly. "You have come back to your inheritance, and will be agreeably occupied for some time in setting it all to rights again, just as you remember it used to be. And I realise, of course, that you will most likely wish Mama and myself to find another home. Now that I shall have means of my own, there should be no difficulty in that, beyond deciding exactly where we would like to settle."

He stood up, pacing about the room for a little before turning towards her again. "Do you wish to leave the Manor?" he asked, brusquely.

"Why no! I don't dislike living here, if that is what you mean—quite the reverse, in fact. But if you are to live here permanently yourself, you will naturally want us to go."

"I see nothing natural about it. I don't wish you to go."

"Well, that is very generous," she said, uncertainly, "and of course, I am grateful—Mama, too, I'm sure. But I don't quite know—"

"What don't you know?"

She shook her head, evidently reluctant to answer.

"Well?" he persisted. "If you did not object to living side by side with me when I was merely your tenant, surely you could not object now that you know we have a closer relationship?"

"That's just it—we were strangers then—"

"And I could be expected to keep my distance? Is that what you would say?"

She made no reply, lowering her eyes so that she could avoid meeting his challenging look.

"Well, you are right," he said, after a pause, almost fiercely. "I shouldn't keep my distance. I don't want you to leave the Manor, Diana, I want you to stay as its mistress and help me to make it into the splendid home it could be. I love you, my dearest girl, with a love all the stronger because it grew out of hatred. Oh, I know that I shouldn't be saying this at present, so soon after that other fellow's false protestations! And no doubt if I were more skilled in such matters, I would give you more time, make myself agreeable to you by a score of gallant attentions, make pretty speeches, try to win your love before I told you of my own—"

She looked up at last, a twinkle in her eye and a blush on her cheek. "But that would be such a dreadful waste of time," she said, in a teasing voice.

"You mean I haven't the remotest chance, no matter what I do?" he asked sombrely.

"No, I don't mean that. I mean—" her voice sank almost to a whisper—"that you don't need to put yourself to so much trouble. I—I fell in love with you at Letty Rathbone's ball, though perhaps I never realised it until Sidney Chalfont tried to make me believe that you had attempted to murder me."

He made some inarticulate sound and, covering the distance between them in a single stride, swept her into his arms. She came readily to his embrace, and for a long time they clung together as though they would never part.

The door opened, and Lady Chalfont came into the room. She stopped at the threshold unable to believe the sight before her eyes.

"Diana!" she exclaimed, in horrified accents. "My dear child! Really, this is no way to behave with a tenant! I knew we should never have taken one."

RONA RANDALL